JIM NASH

Jim Nash The Beginning
Pirate Cay
Thrill Kill Jill
Greetings From Key West
Lost Paradise
No Angels
Mexico Gamble
No Picnic
Fallen Angels
Vendetta
A Girl's Best Friend
Dead End
No Harbor
Dog Days
Startup Blues
Last Stop To Nowhere / The Last
Goodbye
Revenge Is Justice
Escape
Wedding Bell Blues
Snap Brim Fedora Caper
Breakdown
Little Girl Lost
Forget Me Not
All The Glitter
Mexico Time
Partners In Crime
Shop Till You Drop
Lobo
No Free Ride
Gone
Stealing America
Blame It on Djibouti
No Escape
Trouble in Paradise
Nash & Delaney Collide

SEASONAL

Trick or Treat
Helping Santa

JIM NASH INVESTIGATES

The Snap Brim Fedora Caper
The Lady in White
The Lady in Yellow

Print books

Jim Nash
Jim Nash The Beginning
Gun Crazy
Gun Crazy 2
Gun Crazy 3
Fallen Angels
Last Stop to Nowhere
Revenge is Justice
Escape / Forget Me Not
Wedding Bell Blues / Breakdown
Mexico Time
No Free Ride / Gone
LOBO
Stealing America
Blame It on Djibouti
No Escape
Trouble in Paradise
Nash & Delaney Collide

Harry Delaney Adventures
Dead Reckoning
Lie Cheat Steal
Uncharted
Go-Around
Sand Storm
Harry Delaney Collection

Frank Ross Biker Tales
No Way Out
Bad Girls
Bank Robber Dames

Other
The Last President

JIM NASH

NO FREE RIDE

PX DUKE

JIM NASH

NO FREE RIDE

For family, friends, and other miscreants.

Chapter 1

Jim Nash strolled into the coffee shop and scanned the room. It was force-of-habit because of his years spent as a big-city cop. The old habit remained with him, even now, in his PI days.

The line was thankfully short. While he waited, he considered an iced coffee, thanks to the heat wave of the past few days. He threw that idea out almost as soon as it occurred. Drinking cold coffee would be like drinking warm beer. Who wanted that?

Besides, there was too much of the same back at the office if he wanted it—the cold coffee, that is. Not the beer.

The woman was at the counter, sitting on a stool. She was swinging back and forth. His eyes flicked up and back down. She had nice legs. Hands played with the napkin dispenser. She fumbled it and it slipped from her fingers and banged onto the counter. Sunlight shining through the window at her back reflected off the wall to his right. The chrome napkin dispenser flashed, momentarily blinding him.

Still waiting in line for his turn at the counter. Not meaning to, he caught a reflection in the napkin holder. He looked away. Looked again. He didn't recognize the woman. Hadn't noticed her before this. Who was she keeping tabs on? Was she tailing him? It couldn't be. She was there before he arrived.

His turn to order came. He reached into a pocket and paid. When he looked up, the woman was gone. Disappeared. He ambled to the door for a look-see. Meant to check in both directions. The barista called his name. By the time he made the door a second time, the woman was gone for good.

It all reminded him of another woman. It was years ago. Lucy. She managed the dog grooming business at the end of a strip mall. He lived upstairs at the other end of the building until he resigned from the city's police department and left town. It was strange that thoughts of Lucy would come to him. She hadn't crossed his mind in ages.

He made for the building across the street, pushed the door open, and climbed the stairs to his second-floor office with two cups of coffee. He called up to Maddie and their third-floor apartment. "They were out of those crullers you like."

Maddie's dog, Friday, woofed and met him at the top of the stairs. The dog paced back and forth to the office, worrying.

Was the dog trying to warn him about something? Couldn't be. It was still early in the morning. "Friday. It's too early. Go lie down."

Like the dog would listen to him. Maddie made

sure of that. Woman and dog had stood by him through thick and thin, though. He still wasn't sure why Maddie stayed. Maybe it was love after all. It was for him. He wasn't so sure about her.

Friday waited at the office door. The wary dog made certain to be the first to enter the room.

The woman from the coffee shop was sitting on the sofa. Cool as a cucumber. Waiting in the Miami heat and humidity.

It was another bad hair day, as Maddie liked to call them, before she chased him out of the upstairs apartment above their office to pick up the morning ration of coffee.

"Hello. Can I help you?" he asked the woman.

Friday scampered up the stairs to his mistress.

Maddie called down. "Jim? I'll be down in a sec."

Friday woofed to hurry his mistress to where the dog thought she should be. When he finally convinced her to his satisfaction, the pair entered the office almost together. The dog was a mere body length ahead of her. He wanted his mistress to be safe with the stranger in the room.

"Oh. Jim. Who is this? A client?"

Not yet. As far as he knew. Then it came to him, all of a sudden. Lucy. He collapsed in the chair behind his desk.

"No. This is, this is—Lucy? What are you doing here? I thought. They told me. You were dead. How long have you been here? In Miami. Do you live here now? What happened up north?"

It all came rushing back as he stared at the suddenly familiar woman sitting across from him. Had she been tailing him? If she was, he was getting sloppy. Why was she back in his life? What did she want? Did she want anything? Or was she just saying hello because she saw the sign hanging in the window on the second-floor office?

He discarded that as unlikely.

The van rollover. Lucy was ejected. The first thing he did was check her pulse when the dust settled and he could crawl out. The woman didn't have a pulse. She was dead.

Maddie looked from one to the other. Confused. She didn't look happy at the prospect of another woman from the man's past. She went to sit at her desk.

Friday wasn't amused. He went to his bed. Stayed sitting. Kept a concerned eye on the stranger his mistress's man appeared to know. He doggie-sighed and settled onto his bed and crossed his forepaws.

The dog, if he was able, might sense that it was going to be a long day.

Chapter 2

Maddie **got up and** walked from behind her desk to stand in front of the woman occupying the sofa. Towered over her. She hesitated before finally holding out her hand. "Hi. I'm Maddie. Jim's partner in the business." She didn't admit to being his partner in anything else. She didn't have to. It hung over her words like an anchor. She didn't back off to allow the woman room to stand.

"I'm Lucy. Pleased to meet you."

The woman's reply didn't come fast enough.

Maddie withdrew her proffered hand. She was nice about it. If nice was the word for such a display. Even Jim noticed.

Maddie was laying down the law. Marking her territory.

It was all right by him. At this stage of his life, he recognized he needed a woman to do things that way. Needed Maddie to do it.

Even so, he knew, too, that he needed to find out what the hell was going on. What the hell had been going on.

"Are you doing to tell me—tell us—what you're doing here? It's been a long time, Lucy," Jim said.

The words were forming on his lips. Lucky Lucy. He snapped his mouth shut and instead thought back. How many years? The woman from the coffee shop was older. Filled out. He supposed he was, too. Muffin-top. He remembered her saying it. And dead. She didn't say that. He did. To himself. Lucy was dead. Maybe not today. But she was back then.

He looked up at Maddie. He didn't have to explain. Thank goodness. He had told Maddie the whole story. Once he got to know her. Pillow talk. He figured it was only right that Maddie should know what a lady-killer he was.

An actual lady killer, that is. Not the romantic kind.

Maddie's shrug seemed to acknowledge it all. She returned to sit in the chair behind her desk. Wanting to put something between her and this interloper. Swiveled to face the stranger. Except the woman wasn't a stranger any longer. She was face-to-face with the woman Jim told her about. She was face to face with a dead woman.

A reluctant Friday sat up in his bed. He sensed he wouldn't be going for that walk after all.

"That's a friendly dog. Is he yours?" the woman back from the dead asked.

Maddie nodded.

Friday's ears perked up at the sounds coming out of the stranger's mouth.

"His name is Friday," Maddie said.

"What happened with Zelda, Jim? Did you look after her?"

Maddie stood up. Her chair bumped against the wall. "I think I'm going to leave you two to get caught up. Come on, Friday. It's time for our walk."

Friday wasn't so sure. He looked up at Jim. Then at Maddie. And finally, at the new female in the room. In his room. He snorted his displeasure before making for the door, where he halted to wait for his mistress. She didn't appear to be in any rush.

Maddie was almost at the door.

"I think I'd like you to stay, Mads," Jim said.

Maddie looked across the room at him.

"I want you to stay."

The second time, it was more forceful. Maddie returned to her desk.

Friday dutifully followed his mistress and settled on his bed. He let go with another sigh. Walk. No walk. He wished his mistress would decide, one way or the other.

"You don't owe me any explanations, but what are you doing here, Lucy? What do you want? Is there something we can do for you?" He emphasized the we. Wanted to make it plain he and Maddie were more than just business partners.

"First, my name isn't Lucy. It's Evelyn. Evelyn Payne."

Jim swung his chair to face the woman square on. "Of course. Your identification was a fake when I pulled it out of your bag." He remembered the exact moment he checked it. "Don't stop now."

Her ID had looked good. He should have

known. He saw enough fake IDs. It had to be feds if the fake fooled him, and it definitely did that.

The woman went on. "I work for the Federal government. I came here to ask for your help."

Jim sighed and looked at Maddie again. Where and from whom had he heard those words before? This woman wasn't intent on bringing her life into the present. She was intent on bringing his life back to the past, whether or not she knew what she was doing.

"I'm from the government and I'm here to help, comes to mind, Evelyn. You're going to have to do better."

"Call me Evie, please. Evelyn sounds like an old woman's name."

Jim took notice as Maddie fidgeted in her chair and looked at the clock. "Just get to it before dark, all right?" he insisted.

"Well—"

Jim interrupted her immediately. "One more thing. Will the help be on your behalf, or on behalf of the government?"

He was already through that wringer more than a time or two. It hadn't worked out in so many ways he couldn't count them all.

"It will be both."

He held up a hand for her to stop. "Maddie, would you mind printing out the standard contract for 25 a day plus expenses? The one with the rider for your services, if required. You know which bank to include."

Evelyn looked confused. "Twenty-five a day? That's hardly—" Evie looked from Jim to Maddie.

Her eyes settled on the dog. Neutral territory.

"It's not 1946, Evie. It's 25 hundred a day. If Maddie is required, it will be plus another 25 a day." He wanted to shut Evie down. The faster, the better.

"We will need twenty-five thousand in advance before I even listen to you."

That was the only way he knew how. He was pretty sure she'd have to make a phone call. If whoever was on the other end of that call didn't agree—

"I can't authorize that. I'll need to talk to someone first."

He was right. "Where are you staying?"

Evie gave up the name of a boutique hotel he recognized.

"If the money is in the account, we'll see you there at 0800 tomorrow. If it isn't, we'll wait until the next morning, same time. Understand?"

The response had the desired effect. Evie adjusted her position on the sofa, getting ready to stand. "Yes."

The woman got up to leave. Friday sat up so fast he had to be listening in like he understood every word. He looked from Maddie to him and back. He ignored Evie.

"You've got three days, Evie. No money, no Jim Nash and company."

Maddie slid the contract across the desk and followed Evie to the top of the stairs. She waited until the woman descended and stepped into the street.

"What the hell was that about, Nash?"

He had no idea, and that's what he told her. "I'm

hoping the rate is so off the wall she won't be able to convince the higher-ups to sign on. What do you say we pick up some Chinese and I'll tell you again about Lucy?"

"You mean Evie."

"Yes. Whatever it is she's calling herself these days."

It could be their last meal together for a while, or a first on this job. He didn't tell Maddie that. "There's one more thing, Mads."

Chapter 3

Jim opened the office safe and lifted out the black hood with both hands. It bulged with the cash he had rescued from the cartel safe house in Matamoros, thanks to Nancy Boyle and Luz. He dropped it on the desk. It landed with a thud.

Maddie took one look. "I hope there aren't any heads in that thing, Nash."

He opened it and dumped the proceeds on the desk. "There's over 300K sitting there, and I have a plan."

She got up and closed the office door. She twisted the lock and it clicked into place. "I'll bet you do. So that's what you were doing down there with Nancy and Luz? Looking for spare change? Pull up a chair, Friday. This is going to be good."

Friday looked up at his mistress. His ears twitched.

Jim said, "Not exactly. I happened to trip over a little of it. I found it in one of the houses we were checking out to find Luz."

Neither Nancy nor Jim knew where Luz got to since her return in Nancy's jet, as he called it. They were both puzzled by her absence. Per his promise, he didn't tell Maddie that Luz was Nancy's daughter. He didn't tell anyone. It wasn't for him to say.

"About that—" Jim shook his head. What happened in Mexico stayed in Mexico, as far as he was concerned. Besides, he wasn't ready. He went on with his plan. "I think we should slide 50K in Emma's direction. What do you think?"

It didn't fool Maddie. "We? Who is this we you speak of?"

"That's we as in you and me, dear. You're as much a part of this business as I am."

He already knew Maddie wouldn't let up.

"So you're saying we should donate to Emma?" she asked.

"Yes I do," he said. "Call it incidentals if you must. Setting fire to the van. Helping us out in all the ways she does with Tricia and Nancy and Don. Babysitting Friday. All the good stuff."

Maddie didn't hesitate. "She could use the cash. She needs a new car—"

"I'm not sure she should haul it out for something like that. Maybe the company can front a vehicle for her instead. But she still gets the 50K, all right?"

Maddie got up from behind her desk.

"Not a problem with me. I think she's home. I'll go get her. Come, Friday. Let's go see Emma."

Jim began stuffing the money back into the hood. He counted out 50 in bundles. When he finished, he returned the rest to the safe and locked it. He left the office door open.

Friday bounded up the stairs ahead of his mistress. He was always excited to see Emma. She had better treats than his mistress usually did, especially if he showed up at Emma's door when she was eating breakfast.

Toenails scraped on the floor as the big dog skidded to a halt in front of Emma's door. He barked once. That was usually all it took for Emma to open it. This was no exception.

Emma said, "What are you doing here, Friday? It's not breakfast. Are you looking for trouble?"

He scampered past the woman's legs and sat down at Emma's feet. The dog's tail swept the spotless floor as Emma's fingers found an ear and scratched.

"Hey, Mads. What's up?"

"Jim and I would like to talk to you if you have time."

Friday took the lead down the stairs. Emma followed. Maddie brought up the rear. When everyone was in the office, she locked the door.

Emma turned as it clicked into place. She looked concerned. "What's going on? Is Tricia all right? Is someone in trouble?"

Jim's grin was so big he could hardly move his lips. "Did Maddie tell you?"

Emma took in the pile of cash on the desk. "What's up with that?"

Jim's grin didn't go away. "Have we got a deal for you, Emma." He explained how he appreciated her help in every way. Dumping the van. The trips out of town to the marina with Tricia. Standing by Don and Nancy. Standing by him and Maddie.

"Maddie and I think the company should front a car for you. Or an SUV. Anything you want. We considered giving you 50 thousand, but you wouldn't be able to buy a car with it, if you get my drift."

Emma looked from Jim to Maddie. "I understand what you mean. But a car? Can you afford it?" She eyed the pile of cash on Jim's desk.

He went on. "So—" He slid the bundle across the desk. "Here's the 50 anyway. You get that, and a company car." He could see the wheels turning.

"Are you sure, you guys? Business has been that good? Not that it's any of my business."

He had to make one thing perfectly clear. "You can't put it in a bank account. A safe deposit box would be good, though. Maybe in two different banks. Just in case, you understand."

She nodded furiously before collapsing on the office sofa. She understood. "I never— it was all fun— you don't—"

Maddie interrupted. "Yes, we do. It's settled, Emma. Just don't tell Don about setting fire to the van until he retires."

The women giggled, and Friday barked like he understood. He had been there with Emma, after all.

Jim headed for the door. "I'm off to pick up some takeout. I'll see you all upstairs. Don't forget to put that back in the safe until Emma gets the bank box, okay?"

Emma grinned, reached across the desk, and peeled a hundred from the stack. She waved it in

Jim's direction and handed it off. "Takeout is on me, folks. Keep the change."

Maddie and Emma and Friday headed up the stairs to the apartment to wait for Jim.

An excited Emma could hardly contain herself. "I can send some of my money to dad and Janine now. They'll be thrilled to know they can go on that vacation they've been talking about. You don't know how happy the two of you have made me to be able to help my dad and Janine."

"You deserve it, Emma. I don't think it would be a good idea to mention anything about it to Anya, though."

"I know. She's a chatterbox, but she means well."

"Of course she does. Did you know she was planning on moving out?"

Emma shook her head. "I didn't know that."

"By the end of the month, if I remember. What do you think about us offering her place to Luz?"

"I don't have a say in that."

"Yes, you do. You're part of the family, whether or not you like it."

The two chattered on while they waited for Jim to show up with the food. An hour went by, and then part of another. An anxious Friday waited by the door.

"Wherever did that man get to? He should be back by now."

Emma was quick to pile on. "He better not go far. He's got my fat hun in his pocket."

"If he's gone on the lam, he's going to need more than that before I catch up to him," Maddie said.

The women laughed.

Jim didn't make for the restaurant right away. He had a change of plan. At the last minute, he called for a car to take him to Evie's hotel. He inquired at the desk, but they never heard of her. He gave them Lucy's name as best as he could recall, but she hadn't checked in under that name, either. Disappointed, he made for the concierge and slipped him a fifty before describing Evie to him.

"Not a problem, Mr. Nash. I'll let you know."

"Thank you, Henry."

Chapter 4

Maddie's phone pinged.

"Would you check it out, Emma? It's probably Jim trying to explain how he got lost. We should have sent Friday with him."

Emma rolled her eyes.

Maddie grinned. "Maybe he's having an office snooze. His day has been pretty hectic so far."

Friday's ears perked up and his tail wagged. The dog was always up for an office snooze in his favorite sunbeam.

"I declare. That dog thinks he's human."

Emma handed the phone to Maddie. "The text says she's not registered at the hotel. Who's not registered?"

"So that's why he's not back. We had a new client come in earlier. Something about a government job of some sort." Maddie went on the tell Emma the story about dead Lucy-now-Evelyn-call-me-Evie because Evelyn sounded old.

"What the hell?" was all Emma could say after she listened to the story.

"I know. Some people just won't stay dead. Anyway, he's putting it to them for 25 a day plus. Ten days in advance. He gave her a contract to sign. Evie has three days to agree or disappear for good."

Maddie's phone rang. She looked at the number and picked up.

"Maddie? This is Javiar at the—"

She recognized the name immediately. The man was one of their informers, albeit on an irregular basis. "I know, Javi. What is it? Are you okay?"

If they needed information on a guest at the hotel where Javi worked, he was their man.

"It's about Jim. I just saw him being hustled into a black van by two men and a third that looked to be a woman. They were all wearing masks."

"Holy crap. We're coming right now."

The threesome double-timed it down the stairs and into the Packard. With Maddie behind the wheel, tires squealed as the old car dodged traffic and careened around corners. The car screeched to a halt in front of the valet parking at the high-end hotel.

"Wait here, Em, okay? Come Friday."

She attached the long leash and led the dog into the hotel toward Javiar. He wasn't able to tell her much more than he had on the phone. He explained how Jim was looking for a woman who wasn't checked in.

Maddie pulled out her phone. "You mean this woman?"

"I guess. It could be the woman he described. She isn't here. Unless she's been in hiding the whole time."

"A disguise, maybe?" she asked.

"Could be. But I don't recognize her."

"I'm going to walk Friday around the lobby, okay?"

Javiar nodded, and Maddie made sure Friday kept his nose busy. Before long, the pair were back at the Packard, where she found Emma chatting up the valet.

"I got nothing. It looks like you got a date."

"I give him credit for trying," Emma said. "He told me he saw the van and a man being hustled into it by three masked people. One maybe a woman."

Maddie handed over her phone with Lucky Lucy's picture on display. They started to call the woman by that when Jim told her what happened.

"I know, I know. Ask anyway, just in case."

The valet shook his head. Emma handed off a piece of paper to Maddie.

"You're giving me the man's phone number? Just how long has it been since you were last in the game, woman?"

"No, silly. It's the plate number of the van."

"Well. You've def been hired. It's your turn to drive. I need to call Boyle."

Don Boyle promised he'd get back to her as soon as he was able. Only five minutes later, her phone rang. Don's personal number showed on call display.

"What did he do to piss off the feds, Maddie?" Don asked.

"He's charging them 25 hundred a day plus, ten days in advance," she replied.

"In that case it's no wonder they want to get rid of him. They probably found someone cheaper." Boyle chuckled at his joke.

"Nah. According to dead Lucy who's come back to life as Evelyn-Payne-call-me-Evie, he's the only one who can do this job. I'll send you a picture of the woman who might be one of his kidnappers. She's Fed too, I think."

"I swear, Maddie, that man and his women. No disrespect intended."

"None taken, Don. Say hi to Nancy and Trish for us, okay?"

Maddie hung up the phone. "Don says it's a fed van, so maybe he's not so bad off—"

"Yeah, in that case, let's all remember Guantanamo."

It was plain Emma was in a bit of a funk over this latest news.

"Can I ask a question, Mads?"

"Ask away. I have no secrets."

"Do you think we should try to find Luz and let her know? There's an off chance this could be serious. I don't know how well you know her, but I'm pretty sure the woman's latest call to dance in Mexico didn't get both Jim and Nancy down there on a whim."

"You're right. I'm not going to go into what I think happened, because it's too crazy for words. And Nancy? Who would have known? She's still my friend, though. Yours, too."

"So you're saying you don't know how to get in touch with Luz?" Emma asked.

"Pretty much." Maddie opened her burn phone and called Nancy at home. She picked up immediately.

"What is it, Maddie? I haven't heard from you

since my last adventure with James."

"Yeah, sorry about that. Say, we just took a job with the feds for a substantial amount of money."

"Good for you. How is it going?" Nancy asked.

Maddie hesitated. "Well—" She wasn't certain how much to reveal without appearing as though she needed Nancy's help. She dove in anyway. "Jim has disappeared. We think he's been kidnapped. When we went to check out the hotel—"

Nancy interrupted. "Who's we?"

"I asked Emma to come with. We checked out the hotel where he was supposed to meet up with the federal agent and sign the contract. He ended up dumped into a government van by three people."

"How do you know it was government?"

Maddie dodged the question. She didn't think Nancy needed to know Don had helped her.

"Everyone there knows Jim by sight. The valet saw it go down and wrote down the plate number."

Maddie wasn't sure how to proceed. "You know, with that last Mexico thing he went on to find Luz, I'm really worried. I don't know what to think."

Maddie already knew the woman was thinking it probably resulted from their last foray with Luz. "I could have Luz get in touch. She might know something to set your mind at ease." Nancy's response didn't build confidence.

Or most likely, she might not, but Maddie didn't say that, even though she was thinking it.

"Thanks, Nancy. I appreciate it."

<h1 style="text-align:center">Chapter 5</h1>

Jim Nash walked across the front of the hotel. He was headed in the direction of his contact. The van screeched to a halt in front of him. He didn't twig immediately to what was about to go down. By the time he did, it was too late.

The side door slid open and banged against the stop. The open door revealed a crew of three, and instinctively he knew they were there for him.

They jumped to the ground, one after the other. The rush was coordinated to surround him on three sides. That was all it took. A simple push caught him half-stride trying to side-step out of harm's way. All three saw through the maneuver. The push had him off balance. Too late to make a difference, the move forced him into the waiting hands of two mask-wearing individuals waiting in the van. They subdued his arms while a third pulled a black hood over his head and zip-tied his wrists.

He tried to get off a kick. It bounced ineffectively

off of one. They were definitely professionals. He thought he made one as a woman and wondered if it was Lucky Lucy. "You're not winning friends and influencing people, Evie. Not a good idea. The price just went up. A lot."

A man's voice told him to shut up while he continued binding his ankles.

"You were looking for my help. It's going to cost the taxpayer, but you'll still get it. You should have agreed on day one. All this could have been avoided. I might even have come along willingly wherever it is you're taking me."

Exasperated, he shut up. There was no sense antagonizing his abductors. He was counting on his connections with hotel staff. He paid some of them for years for the odd tip he used in his investigations. Nothing too rich, but enough to make sure someone was paying attention. It was something the kidnappers wouldn't know.

Maddie would. Almost as soon as it happened. It would annoy the lot of them when the promised takeout didn't show up. He also knew food would be low on their list of priorities once they found out he was taken.

He settled in for the drive, expecting a long one. It wasn't. Maybe ten minutes. Fifteen, max. The van made noises like it was climbing floors in a parkade. He tried to count levels, but it was impossible, given the number of times he was forced to lean. It meant they were somewhere downtown. The parkade had to be tall.

The van slowed, turned, and then bumped gently against something. A wall, most likely. The front door opened and closed. Steps moved away. Two people. The sliding door opened. More steps. He counted to 30 and removed the hood in time to see someone he recognized getting out of a black SUV.

Of course. Government. That, or what he liked to call a non-government slash drug dealer. Which was it now?

"You're taking a chance, Evie. Our contract just went out the window. The price is two times what I quoted. Furthermore, I won't start before the first installment is deposited."

Tires screeched in the background. The squealing got closer and higher. Either someone needed a spot in the parkade real fast and real bad, or the shit was about to be more evenly dispersed.

"You're into it, Evie. My friends are coming for you. You better disappear before you're the one wearing the black bag."

Brakes squealed and tires skidded to a halt. Almost immediately he recognized the almost silent pfhtt-pfhtt-pfhtt three-burst of a suppressed MP5. Lead collided with parkade wall, scattering cement chips. Evie didn't budge. The look of panic on her face told him she couldn't. She remained frozen in place.

"Don't kill her!" he yelled.

The Packard's door opened. "Get in, Santiago." Luz stepped out.

He turned to Evie. "It looks like your compadres left you hung out to dry, Evie. What are you going to do now?"

He pulled the seat forward and climbed into the back. The door didn't close as he expected. Instead,

Luz sprinted toward the woman.

"Don't kill her, Luz. She doesn't deserve it. Yet. She probably doesn't even know what she's got herself into."

Luz didn't kill her. She turned the tables and pulled a black hood over Evie's head. She patted her down. Removed a phone and tossed it into the van before shoving her toward the Packard. She zip-tied the woman's hands behind her back and pushed her into the front passenger seat beside Maddie. Luz slid in beside her.

Luz kept the short barrel of the HK pressed against Evie's side. It was angled down and back so as not to hit Maddie in the event she needed to pull the trigger.

"Put the top up. The windows are dark enough."

No one spoke. They wove their way out of the parkade and into the street. Luz directed Maddie with hand signals. Eventually, they ended up at a storage facility. Luz got out, punched in a code, and directed Maddie to a unit. She got out again and entered another code to open the door.

Maddie drove the Packard into the cavernous space. It was occupied by plastic storage boxes. A table and chairs. A cot. A fridge and a microwave.

Jim moved to pull the hood from Evie's head.

Luz made her displeasure known.

"Leave it on, Santiago. It is good you care for her. I do not. Neither does your partner."

<h1 style="text-align:center">Chapter 6</h1>

The Packard's trunk popped open. Luz withdrew a water bottle and a thick towel.

Maddie pushed Evie into a chair.

Luz deposited the items in front of the woman. The heavy plastic bottle slammed onto the concrete floor. The water gurgled ominously.

"Now you can remove the hood, Santiago," Luz told him.

Jim pulled the hood off.

Evie blinked. Her eyes moved to take in her surroundings. She glanced down. Spotted the bottle and the folded towel. Immediately, her eyes widened in anticipation of what she knew was coming.

She squirmed in the chair. Shook her head. Tested her bound wrists. There was no doubt. She knew exactly what she was in for. She'd read the old confidential reports and seen enough of the news to know what was going to happen.

Luz dragged the table beside the woman's chair.

She hefted the bottle onto the table and made a show of tipping it on its side. It gurgled again. The sound only served to increase Evie's agitation.

"What are you doing here? Why have you been following Jim? Why didn't you approach him in the coffee shop? Why did you choose to do it in the office with his partner? Why did you try to kidnap him only hours ago? Who were the other people involved in the kidnapping? Are they in hiding? Where did they go?"

Luz's questions went on non-stop. She made sure the prisoner didn't have time to answer.

"What is it you want Jim to do? Are you working for yourself? Are you working for the government? How long have you known Jim was in business here? Did someone you know ask you to investigate his whereabouts? Is it official business? Unofficial business?"

Maddie finally tired of the questioning. "That's enough, Luz. She's not going to talk."

Luz made a show of peeling the top from the water bottle and tipped it. Water gurgled into a bucket and onto the waiting towel inside. She straightened the bottle before pulling the towel out. She partially wrung it out. Water splashed into the tin bucket.

The sound effects put an even bigger scare into Evie. She let out with a sob that echoed through the tin-walled structure.

"All right. All right. My bosses asked me if I knew anyone who had a law enforcement background. I knew Jim left Boston, but I didn't know where he was. Supervisors told me he did some freelance work for the government when he left the city. I didn't know he was down here."

Evie inhaled deeply and went on like her life depended on it. Maybe it did. Luz wasn't looking convinced in the slightest. Neither was Maddie.

"You're wasting our time. What's the deal, and why is Jim the one?"

Jim stepped between the women. "Remember that rate I quoted you the other day? Like, yesterday? It's gone up. It's now five a day, plus. Ten days in advance."

He congratulated himself on turning Emma's big payday into a legal one. Once the money landed in the company account, he could immediately deposit it in full into Emma's bank. If the money lands in the account. There would be no telling after this massive screwup on Evie's part.

"You already know we're better than you and your team. We're not scared of federal agent kidnapping charges. We have your office conversation on tape. It won't look good that you tried to get me to cooperate by tossing me into a van in front of your hotel. Which, by the way, you're not registered in. So you lied to us about that, too."

Jim nodded at Luz.

She reached for the Buck 110 in her belt sheath. Withdrew it. The blade flipped open and locked in place with barely a whisper. Luz forced Evie forward in the chair and sliced through the zip tie in a single motion. Evie's blood-drained hands slipped to droop beside her body. She slowly brought them up and began massaging them.

Jim said, "A token of our goodwill, unlike your

kidnapping effort at the hotel. Next time, don't kidnap someone in front of a business where the employees know the victim like they know me."

Evie settled back in the chair. It appeared as though she was ready to talk.

Maddie and Luz moved off and regrouped beside the Packard.

Evie said, "It's about a massive human trafficking ring. It ranges over the southeastern states. We heard you were involved in a rescue on the Keys. We wanted to know who it was, and why that person was the only one."

They obviously didn't know about the van load of victims he and Don Boyle had freed in back of the Largo Motel. Probably just as well. It would keep his fishing buddy out of it. After Nancy's recent Mexican trip, he doubted very much Don would be keen on becoming involved.

One name came immediately to mind. "Wilson. Leanne Wilson. Was she your informant?"

Leanne Wilson had been a cop with him up north. They both left around the same time. She recognized him in Largo Palms and pulled him over in the RV. In fact, she gave him a warning not to become involved. He made a mental note to get in touch with her before accepting this job. If he ever found out what the job was.

"We're going to drop you at the parkade. Consider yourself fortunate I didn't unleash the women on you. You have no idea of their capabilities. The new deal still stands. Fifty thousand for the first ten days. I reserve the right to increase the rate after that. I'll amend the contract and get it to you at the hotel front desk."

He helped Evie stand up. "You have two days left. Don't forget to check in. From now on, there's no free ride."

The return trip to the parkade took place in silence. The crew dropped Evie off at the entrance. No one cared if her van was still there.

The atmosphere in the Packard was considerably better than when the women set out to find Nash.

"Nash, what happened to our Chinese?" Maddie asked.

"More important, James, what happened with my hun?" Emma asked.

Jim could only shake his head. "Luz, are you going to come over and share the bounty? Emma is buying."

"Perhaps another time. I have some things I need to do."

Chapter 7

Jim deposited the takeout on the kitchen table and went to the fridge to pull out the water jug.

"What's with that, Nash? You on some kind of health kick or what?" Emma asked.

"Don't be picking on us menfolk, right, Friday?"

The dog looked up from his bed and immediately ignored everyone but for the wiggling fingers underneath the table. He recognized who owned them immediately. He went down on his tummy and started his own wriggling toward them.

"The menfolk around these parts need to be of sound mind and body to keep up with you women."

Maddie looked at Emma. They both laughed. "You're kidding, right? After all the time the pair of you spend sleeping in the office?"

An exasperated Jim responded, annoyed that he had been caught out one time—or maybe more. He couldn't count them all. Or remember. "We do not sleep in the office," he insisted. "We merely have the occasional little nap after our runs. Now dig in or I'll take it back."

Jim pointed at Friday. The dog was already halfway across the floor on his way to Emma.

"Who's feeding my dog Chinese? Shame on all of you," Maddie said. "Friday, you are such a little mooch."

Emma grinned when Friday's cold nose found her fingers. She took a bite of chicken from her plate and passed it down to him. He rewarded her with a nudge to her leg.

"No wonder he's so pudgy." Maddie looked across the table at Jim. He held up his hands. "Not me. I'm not pudgy. I've been losing weight."

"You wouldn't be if I let you get under the table with Friday. I'm pretty sure you'd both be happy."

Jim grinned at Friday and the dog's antics.

"Now dear. You know you make me immensely happy, whether you allow me to eat and drink from a bowl on the floor beside Friday or not."

He chuckled at his joke and changed the subject back to the elephant in the room. "What are we going to do about Evie? Do we trust her? If we go along with her story, we're going to need someone to go undercover. There's no better person to do that than Luz. She's already witnessed the trafficking operation firsthand. She was part of it in Largo Palms."

"Yes, but will they recognize her? If they do, she could be in danger. Would we be able to back her up if she needs it?" Maddie asked.

"What I find hard to believe is that the Keys are a hotbed of human smuggling. How are they bringing the people in, by cruise liner? I haven't read about the

Coast Guard breaking anything up. No news reports of boats. No miniature submarines like the ones they use for drug smuggling. Nothing.

Jim tried to remember the last time he'd seen anything on the news or in the few remaining newspapers about large groups of immigrants coming in via the Keys. "I think a little research is in order. Why don't I call my contact in Largo Palms? She's a state trooper I used to work with in the Detective bureau up north before I left."

"How did you run into her?" Maddie asked.

"She recognized me in Boyle's rented camper on our last fishing trip and pulled us over. I'm going down to the office. Come on, Friday. We have an assignment."

A reluctant Friday wheezed from his bed. He was just settling in. He got up, snorted, and looked over at his mistress.

"Don't be giving me snorting side-eye, dog. Go with Jim. He feels the need for some male companionship. And a nap."

Emma and Maddie snickered.

Jim tromped up the stairs behind Friday, who was eager to settle in on his more comfortable upstairs bed. There was no office sunbeam to enjoy when it was dark.

"I found what I was looking for. Leanne—Officer Wilson—was eager to fill me in." He told Maddie and Emma about the human trafficking and smuggling that went on from Bimini as Wilson described it.

"It's only 50 miles offshore. Apparently, it's been a goldmine for drug smugglers and human traffickers for decades. The smugglers don't care about life or loss of it, as long as the boats keep up their back and forth. A sinking or worse isn't a problem for them. They have a never-ending stream of customers and drugs.

An exasperated Maddie interrupted. "Tell me the feds don't expect us to do anything about it, Jim. If the Coast Guard can't control the back and forth, how are we expected to do anything?"

"I have no idea. We're two people. Three if we include Luz in this royal screwup that Evie and her cohorts expect us to take part in. And I might add that Evie's a fed. Surely she must know the score. Let me make some phone calls," Jim said. "I know a guy—"

Chapter 8

Jim Nash returned to the office where he put in a call to Luz. He expected the number was a burn phone. After telling her what he was up to, she agreed to meet at a coffee shop. He arrived early and scouted the place. It was perfect. He took over a four-top in back with a view of the door and the street and waited. He suspected Luz would do the same.

"Santiago."

The familiar voice surprised him. Of course. She had entered through the back door. Same old dependable and reliable Luz. "What is going on? Is everyone all right?" she asked.

Her concern was always for everyone else. He was certain she wanted to think she was our guardian angel. Perhaps she was, although after our latest Mexican sojourn, it was left to him and Nancy to extract her and bring her home safe and sound.

"You scouted the back."

She smiled. Before sitting down, she arranged the

chair to keep eyes on both doors. The outline of her sidearm was plainly visible. She adjusted her shirt and it disappeared.

It took him a while, but he had finally convinced the woman to get her Private Investigator license. Maddie had agreed with him, and Luz was now on our payroll.

"Si. I saw you taking care of the front. Just like you are doing now."

Why was he not surprised?

He went to order two café mochas and returned. For some unknown reason, he had taken a liking to the sweet drink, even though it left him with a white mustache. He took a sip, made a swipe with a napkin and all was well with the world. So far.

"I have a job for us," he announced out of nowhere.

He described how traffickers were using Bimini, 50 miles offshore, as a base for smuggling. How the Coast Guard wasn't even on the edge of the picture. How death and destruction followed the boats running back and forth under cover of night. Sinkings due to weather. Competitors shooting up boats.

Luz listened patiently while sipping at her coffee. "This drink is too sweet, James. It is bad for the waistline."

"You've been spending too much time listening to Maddie talk about my—"

She interrupted mid-excuse. "No. I was thinking about my own, gracias do todos modos. Not everything is about you, Santiago."

"TouchŽ."

"Now we are fencing?"

He held up his hands. "No, no, Luz."

Luz stood to go. "I will check out this Bimini place and get back to you, all right?"

Chapter 9

Jim didn't hear from Luz for three days. No voicemail. No text. Nada. He didn't know if she would be in, or out. When next he saw her, the woman had a bad sunburn and a surly attitude.

"What have you got me into, James?" she asked.

Oh-oh. The Santiago was disappeared. That was trouble. "What do you mean?"

"I crossed to Bimini."

"Wait. What? Bimini? What the hell?"

"I thought I should go to look. I spent three days at a place called the Angler. Bimini looks to me like it is ground zero for what you talked about. In fact, the entire island appears to be ground zero for all of it."

For sure that saved them wasted time scouting. Although, he would have liked to do some of it for himself. He didn't let on.

"This is what that woman kidnapped you for? To help with that?"

He already knew it was an impossible task.

"Her name is Evie. Yes. Although now that you've told me you witnessed it for yourself, I'm not sure what Evie will want. I don't think it's something we can fix. Hell, the Coast Guard can't do anything about the smuggling. It's a drop in a very big bucket."

"I have witnessed it first-hand. You are right. It would be impossible. Boats go out and come back every night. The same boats. There is no rest for any of them. They refuel. They wait until dark. They go out again. The boats come back."

She hesitated.

"At least, most of them. Some do not."

She pulled out more than a handful of 3x5 photos from her bag and pushed them across the four-top before going on. "Do not worry. I printed them myself."

It was like Luz read my mind. Maddie could do that, too. He went through the photos, one at a time, while she went on.

"Perhaps it is on this side where they want you to do something. That would not be so impossible, I think. We saw what was going on in Largo Palms. Perhaps that is one end for the smuggling of the people and drugs."

Luz was making some good points. He couldn't dispute any of it. For sure it would be a lot safer on this side of things. From what he had researched, it would make more sense to do it here. Luz's preliminary work in Bimini would help nail it down.

"You're right, Luz. In that case, we'll need some cars. Beaters. Maybe a van or a step-van." Already Jim's mind was spinning with possibilities.

"Beaters? What do you mean?"

"Ah. You're in for a treat, then. Remember all those old cars you used to see—"

"Oh yes. At home. I know what you mean now. Do you want me to pick them out for you?" she asked.

He thought it important to allow Luz to take part any way she could, notwithstanding her unscheduled flight in and out of Bimini. If picking out some beat-up and rusted out cars might be her thing, more power to her.

"There are still some things I need to sort out first, Luz. Money, for one. We need to get paid up front or this deal won't go down. I'm not going to put us all to work for nothing. In the past, I've had some bad dealings and bad feelings about what the feds got me to do for them. A lot of it was on me, but I'm not about to repeat any of it. Not for anyone."

He pushed back the chair and stood up to emphasize his point. "Not any more. Save your receipts for the flight, hotel, and meals. The feds are going to be picking up the tab for all of this."

He wondered if Luz would have any paper to submit, given her penchant for secrecy. He swept the pictures off the table and gestured with the handful of photos. "Can I keep these?"

She nodded and stood up. They switched out.

Luz departed via the front door.

He walked out the back before making his way to the office. He was greeted by Maddie at the top of the stairs. "Well? Is she in?"

"Is who in?"

Maddie looked at him like she could read his mind. It always made him nervous when she did it.

"Yes. Luz is in."

He filled Maddie in on what he and Luz had discussed. About what Luz witnessed in Bimini. That we could do nothing there. It would be like pissing into a wind.

"She went to Bimini on her own? What the hell is up with that woman?" Maddie asked.

His thoughts exactly, but he said nothing. He didn't ask, either. "She came back with a sunburn and a ton of information. Pictures, too."

He handed over the photos. "These will help identify the boats if any of them are beaching at Largo Palms. If they're not—" He considered. "If they're not, we'll need a boat to check out the overnight activity. I'm not buying a boat. The feds wouldn't spring for one, anyway."

Maddie gave him the Oh come on, Nash look, but he shook his head. "Not gonna happen. Luz and I felt what we witnessed in Largo Palms would be a good place to start. She thinks it's one of the termination points for the smuggling operation—drugs and people. I agree with her."

"You've been doing your homework, Nash."

It wasn't only him. He told her again how Luz already jumped a flight to Bimini and spent three days there. "She saved us a lot of time, Mads. A lot. If she can get a look at some of those boats beaching in the area—"

"I can't believe she took pictures, too," Maddie said.

"I know. That woman is turning out to be a real asset."

Chapter 10

All right, so he still had to get some cash up front for the first ten days of the operation. Luz already spent money on her trip. The beaters would be next—if Evie ever came up with the money.

It was turning into a waiting game. Whoever could out-wait the other would be the winner. He was damned if his team would end up losing. He already thought about transferring the first 50K straight into Emma's account. He bounced the idea off Maddie.

She didn't have a problem with it. "It makes it a lot easier for her, since it will come straight out of the company account. She'll get to spend it any way she wants."

Earlier they had discussed giving Emma a lump sum, cash from what he called the savings account stashed in the office safe. Emma wouldn't be able to bank it or send it home. In fact, it would end up a hassle to pay out cash for her living expenses.

"We've been using her a lot. I think it's only fair. You know she's going to go through the roof if it happens," Maddie said.

First thing in the morning, Maddie checked the company account. "It looks like Evie has been busy. She came thorough, and we have a new balance. It's a fresh 100K. There's an email, too. You were right. Largo Palms it is."

Maddie immediately transferred the 50 into Emma's account. They didn't tell her. It would be a pleasant surprise. And surprise it was when they heard the scream. Friday jumped up, immediately concerned for his bestie. He trotted to the closed door and barked.

Jim let him out to scamper down to Emma's apartment. He barked again and scratched at her door.

"Woo-hoo, Friday. We have liftoff. Come on in for a bacon snack."

Jim caught Friday's guilty look over his shoulder before he ducked into Emma's place. The door closed shut behind him.

"I swear, Nash, that woman spoils my dog worse than you."

He was happy. They had the money. All that remained was getting to Largo Palms in the beaters. Which reminded him. "I'm going to ask Luz to pick out some used cars for us. Reliable, yet rusted and worn down. Kind of like me at times." He grinned at her.

"Whatever you say, master. Now let's get busy

and pack a bag. Friday is going to stay with Emma, right?"

Neither of them thought the dog should be involved in the operation. If they needed to move fast, putting Maddie's dog in danger wasn't a part of it. If anything happened to her pride and joy—and he didn't mean himself—she'd skin him alive.

If he was still breathing.

L uz showed up with her beater.
Jim dragged Emma down to tease her about her new car. She wasn't happy, but the frown turned upside-down pretty quick when he explained what they were trying to do. She got in a good shoulder-punch that caused his entire arm to ache.

"Don't lose the receipts if you have any, Luz. The government is going to pay us every dime for this madcap adventure of theirs. And then some."

He grabbed Maddie, and they were off to pick up another car and an extended-box van before returning to the office.

The black SUV pulled into a spot halfway down the street as they returned.

"Speak of the devil. Here they are."

A convoy of black-suit types exited and advanced toward them. It was entirely unexpected. Luz was concerned. "I'm not armed. I wasn't expecting this, Santiago."

"We should be good. Let's get ourselves upstairs where the guns are. Just in case."

Three of us hightailed it to the office. Maddie called up to Emma to keep Friday with her. With the gun safe open, they settled on clip-ons and short magazines. That was all right by him.

He turned around to look for Luz. She wasn't to be seen.

Four federal-looking gentlemen in dark suits entered the office. The disdainful looks on their faces told me our digs didn't impress them. The man with the briefcase set it on Maddie's desk and opened it.

"We have made changes to your contract," stiff upper lip announced.

Maddie looked at me, unsure what to expect.

Jim said, "I'm sorry, gentlemen, but the contract stands as it is. No contract, no deal. Go find your minions somewhere else. I'm pretty sure you must have half a dozen, at least."

He sat down, put his feet up on the desk, and looked up at the government's best before going on.

"The Coast Guard isn't making a dent in Bimini smuggling operations. The only thing slowing the smugglers is the occasional boat that sinks. From what we've heard, it's replaced almost immediately. For an island with a population of 2,000, you're not doing such a great job. And now you want to dump it on us because you think we don't know what's going on."

He drew and breath and hesitated.

"What's it going to be? Do you want us? If not, get out. Now."

He didn't think it smart to let them know they'd already been to Bimini and had witnessed the problem in person. He also didn't think it wise to tell them they had circled the beaters and were planning on heading to Largo Palms now that the money had dropped. And he sure didn't let on that they had an advance in hand.

"Maddie and I are the ones who'll be taking on the assignment. If you have any last-minute information or instructions for us, now would be the time to let us know."

They didn't. Right away, he knew they wanted them to fail. Would it make them look good? Who knew what they were up to? The private help certainly wouldn't look good if the press got wind of it. From there, well, anyone's guess would be as good as his.

"All right, Nash. You win. The contract stands." He tossed the paper across the desk. I allowed it to slide to the floor without looking.

"You need to know I'll be reviewing that to make sure it's the original," he warned him.

"Don't worry. It is."

"I'm not worried," he said. "I'll check anyway. Remember one thing."

He made them wait while he looked at all four of the men.

"No money, no laundry. Now get out."

Chapter 11

Jim called up the stairs to let Maddie know he was taking Friday for his walk. "We'll be stopping at the usual place on the way home."

"In that case, bring some back for me. Emma, too."

He allowed Friday to take the lead with his long leash. They were passing the ice cream store when he halted. He called to the dog. "What do you think, Friday? Will Luz want to move in with all of us in the same building?"

The dog's ears perked up at the woman's name, but he was pretty sure Friday didn't have an opinion. He was contemplating that when a car pulled to the curb in front of them. A woman got out. He recognized Evie.

So did Friday. He tugged at the leash and almost pulled him to his knees in his fervor to get to her.

"Friday. Heel."

He obeyed, reluctantly. He remained tensed. His

eyes stayed on the woman.

Jim knew from the dog's posture he was ready to pounce. "Friday. Sit." He refused. That was a first. What was he seeing that he couldn't?

"What do you want, Evie?" Jim asked.

"I heard some of my people visited you in your office today."

Big surprise. It wasn't. "I haven't reviewed the contract yet. When I'm finished with it, I'll let them know."

He told her about Largo Palms. That her crew was content to allow us to head down. That confirmed his suspicion that Bimini to Largo Palms was the pipeline. Or one of them, at least. Probably one of many.

Evie didn't need to know they were ready to go and that one of his team was already in Largo Palms. He also didn't mention they'd scouted Bimini and decided it wasn't where they needed to be. He didn't say anything about the photos of the boats, either. There was no sense in playing all their cards.

Evie remained wary of Friday. She didn't come closer.

Jim said, "You never told me what you were doing in that dog shop business up north. Were you on a stakeout? If you were, I knew nothing about it."

"Yes, you're right."

She wouldn't say more. "Something about drugs?"

She nodded. "I can't tell you more. It's ongoing."

Ongoing after all these years? He had a hard time believing that. Either the feds were completely incompetent, or there was something else to it. He didn't care. He was far removed from that and happily so.

"Is there something else you wanted, Evie?" Jim asked.

Friday growled. The hair on the back of his neck stood up. He was prepared to leap.

He didn't say a word. He had worked with the dog for a long time. If his instincts told him something, he knew he was probably right.

Evie backed away slowly toward her car.

Friday stayed still. He only relaxed a little. "Good boy, Friday. Good boy."

He went down on a knee and gave him pats and a treat for his efforts on his behalf. "Good boy. I think our walk is over."

He had hardly noticed they made it as far as the ice cream shop. Even Friday missed it.

"Well, look at our good fortune. I think we should get some ice cream to go. What do you think, faithful dog?" Jim asked.

Faithful dog thought it was all right, too. He was a little stand-offish when forced to walk home without a sample tasting. That only lasted until we got upstairs with Maddie and Emma.

When he spoiled one, he liked to spoil them all at the same time.

Jim didn't mention he'd bumped into Evie. There was no sense stirring the pot. That she was tailing at least one of them was obvious. He was glad he had brought Luz into it now. She would be the unknown.

Still, he had to wonder what was going on in the background that they needed to be kept under surveillance.

Chapter 12

Jim and Maddie sat down with Emma and refreshed her memory regarding the fifty thousand. They explained what was transferred to her bank account was legal tender. That it wasn't the shady fifty in cash he originally told her about.

The huge grin on her face said she was happy. It would mean she could transfer money from her bank directly to her father without worry.

He briefed Emma on where they were going and left her the keys to the Packard. He explained it was a rolling armored truck minus a roof. "It drives like a tank until you get accustomed to it. Maybe you could drive it around the block a time or two after we leave. You know, to get accustomed to its idiosyncrasies."

"Nah. It sounds like it handles like a snowplow. I'll be fine."

Jim was happy with that. Besides, it was probably true. Emma had learned how to drive one of those huge blowers at her father's knee when she was a little girl. What could be so difficult about the Packard?

Jim said, "We're going to head out tonight. Luz is already down there scouting the place. That's for your ears only."

Emma voiced a quick, Understood.

"There are loaded rails and a spare MP5 in the office gun safe. There's an office Model 17 and one standard mag. The rest are my specialties. You know, if you need anything."

She looked at him like he was nuts.

"This is for your ears only, too. I briefed Harry at the gun shop about you. He knows you're an employee. If you need anything, he'll trust you on my behalf. Just don't screw up my deal with Harry."

He looked at Emma carefully. She didn't appear to have questions. He asked anyway.

"I think I'm good, Nash," Emma reassured him. "I've already got a burn phone up and running for you guys. I'll take Friday to the kennel for the duration. You called Dr. Hannah already, right?"

Friday snorted and got up from his bed. He recognized the kennel word. He recognized Dr. Hannah, too.

"Oh-oh. Here comes trouble," Maddie said.

The dog looked from Maddie to Jim to Emma and snorted.

"He's not happy."

He reached for the dog, but he wouldn't come.

Instead, Friday sat down by his mistress. He stayed just beyond her reach, too.

"He's pissed," Maddie said. "He likes Dr.

Hannah, though. He'll be all right. She treats him just like he was her own. I think she even takes him home at night."

With that out of the way, he and Maddie were good to go. "We're staying at the Largo Motel. You remember it, right?"

Emma nodded.

They made their way downstairs.

Friday condescended to allow us to pet and scratch, and his tail wagged up a storm.

We all climbed into Emma's Jeep. It wheezed and started. Friday stuck his cold nose against the back of Emma's neck and she giggled. He did it again for good measure.

Emma knew the routine. "Friday. Bad dog."

Jim monitored their six as Emma drove each of us to the beaters Luz had picked out. She did her job well. Rust and squeaking doors and almost bald tires and a trunk full of weaponry greeted each of us.

"Luz did good, I'll give her that. Take care, Emma. We'll be in touch."

Maddie and Jim met in the Largo Palms diner parking lot. The customers were all turned over to a new fishing season. The wait staff and the cook were new, too. My former big-city police partner, Leanne Wilson, was sitting at a four-top in the back. They ambled over and he introduced Maddie.

"I wondered when you'd get here, Nash. It's been a long wait for something to happen."

She brought us up to date on the goings-on of the

traffickers. Told us about the steady armada of boats arriving offshore. How they offloaded onto smaller boats for the return to shore up and down the Keys.

"I'm having a hard time understanding how the Coast Guard can't seem to do anything about an island with 2,000 people being used as a smuggler's paradise. Who are those guys paying off?"

He was careful about his intentions. Other than the traffic stop, the last time he was down here with Don Boyle, he'd not heard hide nor hair from Wilson. That she was a trooper in south Florida surprised him. He played his cards close and didn't divulge one thing more than he had to. That was the whole point of the operation, was it not?

"Do you think you'll be here long, Jim?" Wilson asked.

He wondered who leaked that they were even coming. he eyed Maddie and thought he could see the same question on her face. How were they supposed to be undercover if the local cops knew they were here?

"We don't know. We only know what we've been told about what's going on. I think someone must have told the powers that be we were down here a while ago. They tried to get us to come back on the cheap."

Which wasn't a lie, at least.

"Well, we're glad to have you. You can count on that," Wilson said.

Leanne got up to leave.

"Be sure to stay in touch. If you need anything, let me know. It was nice meeting you, Maddie." Wilson made for the door and the familiar cowbell clang.

"What the hell was that about, Nash? She just let us know our entire operation is blown."

"It would be if Luz was with us. I don't like anything about this. Up to now, I thought it might be a walk in the park. Now I think we're going to have to get a boat and get ourselves dirty. There's no way we can do this from land."

"Do you think Wilson and crew might be doing something illegal? How many know about us and are glad to have us, as she said?"

"Yeah, I caught that too. I think she might have slipped up," Jim said.

Chapter 13

Jim was concerned that Wilson appeared to know all about the operation. They were never told they'd be working with the troopers. It was never presented as an option. That Leanne was waiting for them in the diner said there was a leak somewhere. It had to be on the fed side. It sure wasn't on theirs.

"We just got here and already I'm worried. What the hell is going on?" Jim asked.

Maddie appeared to be just as concerned. "I don't know either, Nash. We'd best keep our boots on and our magazines loaded. What do you think about some kind of long-term rental on a boat? And I don't want a beater. I want new. Or newish, at least. With plenty of horsepower to go with it."

Maddie was right, of course. They'd need a boat. Trying to sort this out from land would be impossible. His burn phone chose that instant to ring. He recognized the familiar accent.

"I have a panga for you. I'll send you the coordinates."

The line went dead. Maddie must have recognized the expression on his face. She looked at me, wanting to know what was going on.

"Luz read our minds from wherever the hell she is. Somehow, she got her hands on a go-fast."

He wouldn't dare ask Luz how she managed it.

"Holy crap, Jim. That woman is not to be trifled with," Maddie said.

"Yeah, don't mess with her, either. She's a stone-cold killer."

He bit his tongue. What happened in Mexico stayed in Mexico. It wasn't up to him to tell Maddie any more than that.

"I'll take your word for it, Nash," Maddie said.

His phone pinged again. It was the coordinates from Luz. "Let's go take a look at our new boat."

Luz was nowhere to be seen when we arrived at the dock. He wondered if she was somewhere ashore monitoring them.

A voice called from the office. "Are you Jim Nash?"

He showed identification and picked up the keys to the huge panga. It was similar to the one he had shared with Luz and Anya during their escapade on the Baja.

The harbor master looked the pair of them up and down. He had to be figuring them for a couple of city rubes out for a weekend getaway. He could see the wheels turning. Two rubes with an overpowered panga would no doubt end up beached on his wharf.

"I haven't seen this one around before. Where did

you pick it up?" he asked.

"A friend picked it out for us. We might buy it if we like it."

Seeing money in a long-term berthing agreement changed the man's attitude. "In that case, enjoy. It's fueled and ready to go."

Jim flashed back to Renaldo on the wharf in Cabo, seeing to the go-fast tied to the wharf. Somehow, he knew the local wharf-rat wouldn't have anywhere near Reynaldo's capabilities.

"Climb aboard, Maddie. We'll take her on a test run."

He powered up the instrument cluster and set a GPS waypoint to *Home*. One at a time, he started the three engines and set them to idle. He checked the gauges. Satisfied with the numbers, he waved to Maddie to drop the lines. She fumbled but she managed to stay dry.

Our getaway was an easy one with the offshore wind. The panga fairly drifted away from the dock. We were off. All he had to do was advance the throttles and steer.

"You can pull up the fenders now. Hang onto the jackline. That's what the line is called that surrounds the cockpit. It'll keep you from falling overboard if you lose your balance."

He caught stink-eye right off. "Aye Admiral."

Jim grinned, and Maddie obeyed, and they were good to go. Past the breakwater, he firewalled the triple throttles, testing their new go-fast. She didn't feel as quick off the mark as César's, but the top speed was equal. He adjusted the plane and gained three or four more knots.

"Your turn, Maddie. Stand with the back of your knees against the seat brace. Use it to steady yourself and you'll be good."

She did as she was told. He made her work the throttles, from bobbing like a cork to full-on for a quick getaway. He demonstrated the plane. He had her switch the bilge pumps on, just in case they were needed, and explained what they did.

"Now hit the *Home* button on the nav panel and watch the action."

He sat back and watched Maddie's face as the boat turned and made toward shore and the wharf where they picked her up.

"Okay, Captain. I'll take over. Have you ever been to sea, Billy?"

"Not on your life, Nash. Now what?"

Maddie moved out of the way and he throttled back. The panga mushed and slowed. As they got closer to shore, he switched off the nav system. It was time for a lesson.

"There are a couple of things you need to know about water depths if you want to stay afloat," he began.

Jim pointed at the depth gage while he explained it only showed how deep the water was beneath the hull and nowhere else. "It can't tell you more than that. There are other ways to see what's going on around you that will help to pick a route in a hurry if you need to."

Maddie looked out beyond the panga. Her head swiveled back and forth. "I can't see anything but what looks like a sandy bottom. I think that's because the water is so clear."

The light breeze and the swell caused the panga to rock gently. Maddie hung onto the jackline for support. She had donned a blue life jacket at some point.

"You can tell the depth of the water by color in a lot of cases," Jim said. "You mentioned the white sand bottom. Well, often that's reflected sunlight from the sand. We're not a sailboat. In fact, this panga is virtually afloat mere inches below the water line."

"So then, if the sand is what I can see, I won't run aground, right?"

"Most likely. Especially in this rig. On the other hand, you might want to keep a watch on what the engines are kicking up at the stern. If there's a lot of sand, you're in danger of grounding them. Make for deeper water before that happens."

Jim advanced the throttles and steered them to another patch. "Here where it's darker could mean there's something close to the surface. Brown, brown, run aground. Could be a rock or a shoal."

It was strange how Rusty's old admonitions came back to him from when she taught me about sailboats.

"Now again, we're not running a keel like a sailboat, so it's not as serious. Still, you could take out a propeller or all three at the same time if you hit anything. If you need all three engines, that wouldn't be good."

She looked around. "What about that green patch close to shore?"

His gaze followed her hand as she pointed.

"Green, green, in between. It could be deep. It

could be grass reflecting green. Or could be shallow." That was almost word for word what Rusty had told him.

"But we're in a flat-bottom panga. Does any of it really apply?" she asked.

That was a good question.

"Well, no. But if a Coast Guard cutter is on your six, you might want to think up a way to lead him aground. And that's our lesson for today."

Maddie gave him a strange look, and he shut up. No sense in telling secrets out of school. School being Mexico, that is.

"I aimed the panga at the breakwater and made for the wharf. When they got close, Maddie dropped the fenders, and they bumped the dock. She made her way haltingly to tie them off. He tossed her the rope for the stern. She wrapped it and tied what looked like a granny knot. She straightened and looked satisfied with herself.

"I'm exhausted," Maddie proclaimed. "I'm heading for the car. You'll find me asleep there, Mr. Admiral."

"Not so fast, sailor. We still have to refuel. We need to check the oil levels in three engines."

"Oh good grief. Can't you hire someone to do that?"

"I did."

"You did?" She sounded doubtful.

"Yeah, no. Not so good. The person I hired is you, *capitán*.

He led Maddie around the panga, showing her the refueling points as they went. He opened up the engine fairings and demonstrated checking the oil on all three, lest she thought checking only one was good enough.

"The three engines are separate except for fuel," Jim said. "You have to be sure we don't forget the oil."

"Aye, Admiral of the fleet," Maddie said. "Chores completed. Now don't bug me. I'm headed to the shop for a beer with the dock *comandante*. If I learn anything of value, I will report back."

"I thought you were going for a sleep?"

"Woman's prerogative. I changed my mind. Haven't you learned anything by now?"

Chapter 14

Jim checked out the panga while Maddie went off in search of cold beer. The nav system was more modern than what Anya demonstrated on our boat on the Baja. Thanks to her efforts in that department, he flipped on the battery and took a better look. Now that they were tied up, he could take his time.

He switched the nav system on and waited for it to stabilize. It picked up the satellites almost instantaneously. He hit the Home button and heard the gyros attempt to position the engines. He selected disconnect and the engines halted their search.

"Wow. It's only been a couple of years and already the systems are so much better." He wasn't speaking to anyone in particular. There was no one around.

"Si señor. Las electrónicas are much better, are they not?"

He was no stranger to that voice. He whirled around to confront Luz.

She welcomed him with a huge grin. Her hair was in a pony tail topped by a baseball cap with the logo of the business on it.

"You've been busy, Luz. And most helpful, as always."

She busied herself with duplicating Maddie's work. She opened the fuel caps and checked the volumes, talking all the while. "Su ayudante—your helper—does a good job, señor."

When she completed that task, she moved to the engines and removed the cowlings to check the oil.

Jim grinned. "I'll be sure to tell her."

Satisfied, Luz finished buttoning up the engines and turned to him. "Where is Maddie?"

He gestured with his head toward the blockhouse at the end of the dock. "She's having a cold one with the wharf manager. I tired her out."

He couldn't help the grin.

"I do not trust him. We will see, I guess. The panga runs good, does it not? And the navigation system is excellent. So modern compared to what we had before."

She, too, was referring to our time on Baja sur and Cabo. It was more than a few years now. Luz was much younger, a mere child.

"I'd say we were lucky back then. I guess we'll find out how lucky we will be this time."

She nodded.

There had to be a reason for Luz to take a wharf rat job. "You must think this is the place," he said. "What have you discovered?"

She looked up at the blockhouse. "I think Maddie is busy working Bud. He is easy if one has a pretty face. So then, many of the smuggler's boats stop here for fuel after their drop-offs at sea. It's a busy place after dark and toward morning as the Bimini crews resupply."

"What about Bud? Is he a part of it?"

"Not that I can tell. He is in it for the money he makes on fuel and oil and food and drink. He sells a lot of everything. I think he's getting rich. He and a few others up and down the Keys."

He wanted to know about the victims, the ones being trafficked.

"As far as I can tell, no people are unloaded here. It's only those needing to fuel."

"So the smugglers unload somewhere at sea."

"I think so," Luz said. "I have scouted other marinas. It appears to be the same for all of them. Empty boats refuel and buy supplies and head back to Bimini. It is quite a routine to see."

Of course it would be. There would be no point in stopping empty boats on their way across the ocean to home.

"Do you recognize any of the boats from the scouting you did on Bimini?" he asked. "Thanks for doing that, by the way. I'm sure it's going to make a big difference."

"Gracias. There are many. I am getting to know the captains too. I pretend I don't speak Spanish. I hear the complaining. They talk about less money for more trips. Overloaded boats. People throwing up. People are desperate to get to America. There are rumors that many of the young women end up in slavery conditions."

He knew about that from what he and Don had

witnessed during their fishing trip. In fact, they had rescued a step-van full of them, thanks to friendly Friday and his *poco* Spanish."

"But they come empty. Sometimes, they wash the boat. Mostly not. The throwing up, probably by the smell."

From what Luz was saying, it was going to be a sea operation. If the boats came in empty, there was nothing to see ashore. It was all taking place at sea. Transfers to smaller boats, most likely. No way did the captains want to get caught with anything suspicious while they needed fuel and oil.

"They come in here with no running lights." Luz looked up at the moon. "In a couple of days it will be *una luna llena*—a full moon. It will make finding where the boats meet up not so hard."

His eyes followed hers. She was right. In these waters, running into unlit boats making transfers could end up killing people.

Maddie walked a crooked path toward the boat. She spied Luz and walked a little faster and a little more crooked. If I didn't know better, I'd say she was drunk. "You have a new dockhand, do you, Nash?"

She didn't recognize Luz in the dim lighting. He wondered if the lighting was dim for a reason, given the only slightly shady business the owner was in.

"Maybe he can help you fuel and oil."

He didn't say a word. Neither did Luz, but he could see the grin beneath the cap.

"I'll tell you all about it tomorrow, captain."

That got a chuckle from Luz and a dirty look from Maddie. He didn't tell her it was Luz. He was saving it.

Jim returned with coffee and breakfast for his captain.

Hung over, she groaned and opened one eye and held out a hand. He put down the food and handed over the coffee. She seemed happy with that.

"You should eat something. We're going to have a long day. And it's starting out a scorcher. Sunscreen and hats work pretty good. Plenty of water."

Maddie groaned and threw the covers off. Two feet hit the floor, and she stood up in too much of a hurry. She lurched and almost fell back into bed. She made a grab for the headboard to steady herself.

"That's it, sailor. That ought to teach you to drink with a landlubber who can hold his liquor."

"Don't remind me. I'm going to take a shower. Did you get us breakfast?"

He gestured to the bags on the table and she hurried off to get wet. When the water turned off, she returned in a robe and sat down.

"Did you get juice?"

He pulled a jar of cold orange juice out of a bag and filled a glass with ice. He made her pour her own.

"Did you get eggs?"

He did the same with a container of scrambled eggs. They were piping hot. He tipped the bag in her direction and made her fish for a knife and fork.

"Good boy, Nash. Wheat toast?"

"Of course. Have a toasted bagel. Is there anything else your heart desires, my princess?"

The remark didn't even garner a dirty look. She was too busy dining on my elegant breakfast.

"Do you remember meeting Luz last night?" he asked.

"What? Luz? No. Where did we run into her?"

he gave her time to think. "On the dock. You thought she was my new dock boy."

Maddie groaned. "No way. That was Luz? Is she pissed at me? I thought she was—"

"Don't sweat it. She was grinning the whole time. And yes, she's our new dock hand. She works there. She's been doing some scouting on our behalf."

He brought her up to speed. "We're going to have to do some night runs in that fastboat to get the lay of the land. We need to know how far out the trades happen."

"The trades?"

"The transfers. Switch-overs. Where the boats that come ashore to refuel unload their cargo. According to Luz, they come ashore empty, which means they unload at sea. After they replenish, they head back to Bimini."

She hesitated before she replied.

"In that case, your captain is going back to bed to get shipshape for tonight. Nudge me when you're ready, Admiral."

Chapter 15

It was time.

Jim nudged Maddie awake.

She groaned, but she threw back the covers. They both knew this was too important to be complaining about anything.

"How's the hangover, girl?"

"I've had worse. The man drinks cheap beer." She yawned.

He grinned. "Of course it was the beer, cheap or not. So, was it worth it? Did you learn anything useful?"

"Yeah, a little. He likes to talk. He's got himself a goldmine if it wasn't for all the other marinas on this side of the Keys doing the same thing. On the good days, he makes regular bank runs with plenty of cash. Gas and groceries with liquor and beer thrown in."

"Can we use him?" he asked. It would save time if they didn't have to boat up and down the Keys looking for a sucker.

"I'd say we are already. He doesn't know what we're doing here, and he's wondering."

He figured on that. It probably appeared suspicious to show up with a fastboat from nowhere. But that's what they wanted. "We'll fix that tonight. I'm not opposed to doing a little refugee smuggling to set him up properly. He'll stop asking questions after that. I talked to Luz about it. We've got a full moon, which is to our benefit given that everyone is running around out there with no lights."

The panga had some kind of radar setup, but it wasn't on a pole to let them see the horizon. It was fixed in the bow. Usability would be extremely limited. They would need to be on top of the swells.

"Why don't you go down and fire up our pride and joy and warm it up?"

"Aye, Admiral. You are one trusting soul if you think I can run that thing by myself," Maddie said.

That was true. But he knew Luz was already on her shift, and she knew all about it. "You'll do just fine. I'll catch you in a bit."

Maddie left, and he headed out to pick up bread and cold cuts and water and some fresh fruit for the over-water picnic. He didn't get any beer for the cooler. He figured Maddie could find her own once she got back to shore and worked the owner of the joint like she did last night.

She had things under control when he pulled the cart across the wharf. The engines were idling nicely in neutral. The GPS was spinning. The nav system was up and running. Even the bilge pumps were engaged. A gentle trickle of water spilled into the berth.

"You did good by the look of it." He wondered how much Luz had to do with it.

Maddie took in the load of groceries. "So did you. What did you bring?"

"It's a surprise for when your stomach starts growling."

He moved to untie fore and aft and stepped onto the fastboat. It rocked gently before settling. he inhaled the salty, clean air brought in by the onshore breeze. The smell was definitely different from what they got in the city.

"I'm ready," Jim told her.

Maddie cranked the wheel, engaged the throttles at idle, and eased away from the dock. She kept us low and slow on the posted limit until we got near the breakwater. She firewalled the throttles and the panga leaped up on its engines. They hit full speed and she worked the plane to gain a few more knots.

Jim leaned into her until his lips found her ear. "You were paying attention yesterday."

"You're damned right I was. I might never get another chance at this. I figure you had your fun down on the Baja. I'm going to have my fun on the Keys."

Except he didn't think they'd be purposefully leading Coast Guard cutters aground, outrunning their skiffs, or launching RPGs at Mexican cartel boats. At least, not right off.

"How's the view forward for you?" he asked. It was pitch black. The almost-full moon was just beginning to come over the horizon.

"It's not so bad. Should I turn my lights off now?" she asked.

Navigation lights were required by law. Red port-side, green to starboard. A white was needed aft.

"Go ahead. Let me know what you think."

It was still early. Any boats they would face were still a long way off. Even those heading out to meet the smuggler's craft were still tied up. He figured they had a couple of hours to kill while they waited.

"Let's get the lay of the land. We need to find out how these boats spot each other and hook up to unload. They can't do it without lights. I'm hoping we'll be able to spot the signals they give each other."

Maddie throttled back. The nav system said they were twelve miles from shore. It was distance enough for a standard fishing boat to pop out and back. Maybe they could make a couple of trips, depending on volume.

He wondered how obvious the Bimini crews wanted to be. Were it up to him, he'd want to put plenty of distance from shore until cargo was unloaded and he had to make way to shore for fuel for the return run.

"Take the wheel, Admiral. I want to see what you brought us to eat."

he was about to open my mouth with something about muffin-tops, but discretion being the better part of valor, he bit his tongue. It hurt, too, but there was no blood. Instead, he called out. "I'll have whatever it is you're having."

They were bobbing like a small cork in the swell. He took the panga out of neutral and set a racecourse a couple of miles long and a mile wide. He set autopilot and the nav system took over with nary a hitch. He sat back in the seat and relaxed, but for keeping watch.

He checked the time. It was getting on to 0300 hours.

"We should be getting some action shortly. Did your drinking buddy happen to mention the times when the action started ashore?"

Maddie was getting nervous. She was constantly looking around, scanning the horizon, on the lookout for other boats. "How are we going to spot the other boats with no lights, Jim? It's dangerous out here if we can't see them."

She was right. It was dangerous. If the number of boats was anything like Luz described, they could be in real trouble. "I'm going to switch on the lights and see what happens. Did you notice anything on that fuzzy radar screen?"

He knew she was too nervous to look, so he bent for a look-see. As soon as our nav lights switched on, the other boats did the same. So that was it. "Finally. Here comes one now."

The captain knew the routine. They were going to be the transport for illegals or whatever else the man had on board that he wanted to dump. He pulled alongside and tossed a rope.

Jim caught it and pulled the boat close.

As soon as the boats came together in the swell, bodies showed themselves and jumped aboard. He counted half a dozen before he pulled away and began making for shore.

"Holy crap. Here comes another one, Maddie. When this one unloads, we def better make for shore."

They took on another half-dozen. They were well behaved. All of them immediately sat down and joined the other six. We were about to find out if Bud was involved in the illegal trade.

Jim powered up and made for home.

Chapter 16

They were into it now with a boatload of refugees.

Jim turned toward shore and firewalled the throttles. He kept their lights on. Other boats flashed theirs in recognition and switched off. Taking the cue, he did the same. He zigged and zagged and hoped for the best in the crowded and overloaded panga.

They weren't so overloaded that they couldn't make speed. Once he was certain there were no boats in front of them, he powered up and put her up on the step. The nav system took them to the breakwater, where he switched it off and manually steered to the dock.

"We're home, Mads. You can drop the fenders."

He shifted into idle and allowed the fastboat to drift against the dock. The wharf rat met them and caught the rope Maddie threw out. She threw out another and the rat tied off the stern.

A dozen illegals jumped up at the same time and tried to climb onto the wharf.

"*Tranquilo. Tranquilo por favor.* Take it easy," he said.

A small van backed its way onto the wharf. Someone got out and the sliding door opened. A man waved. The illegals made their way and were swallowed up. The door slammed shut, and the van took off.

"Now we know. Bud is into it. He had to be watching for us to have that van waiting," he said.

The dock hand moved to refuel the panga.

"Do we need fuel, Jim?" Maddie asked. "We haven't been out that long."

"Si, señora. You need fuel."

Maddie whirled. "Luz!?" She recognized the voice. "Is that you? What are you doing here? I mean—"

Jim couldn't hold it any longer. He broke out laughing. Luz joined him.

"What the hell, you two? What's going on? Was that you last night? Jim? You big jerk. Why didn't you tell me?"

"Oh hell, Mads. Relax. Last night you were intent on finding a beer after our excursion. I didn't want to spoil it for you."

"I'm really sorry, Luz. I thought, I thought—" Maddie looked like she wanted to kick me. Fortunately, Luz interrupted her.

"No problemo, Maddie. I am doing *mi trabajo.* My job. I am the dock hand for now. Just so you know, I do not speak Spanish. *Me entiendes?*"

"I get it, Luz. Nash, you are so in trouble."

"We don't have time. Luz, did you pick up on anything those refugees were saying?"

"Si. They are scared. They don't know where they are going. All have no more money to buy passage."

"So they're screwed. I think we know where they'll end up. Here comes your boss, Luz."

Bud ambled down the dock to join them while Luz busied herself doing her job. She checked the engine oil and hung up the fuel hose before making her way to the shack.

"I brought some cold beer," Bud said. "After last night and the way your partner put it away, I figured she needed some of the hair."

Maddie took one and popped the top before tipping it.

Jim took my own and did the same. "Where are those people going to end up? Any idea?"

Bud didn't look suspicious. He only looked disinterested. "No idea. Once they get into a van, it's not my job. If they don't get in a van, it's not my job, either. I call the police and they take them away."

Jim exchanged glances with Maddie and filed the information away. The next time he crossed paths with Leanne Wilson, he'd be asking her about it.

"Your dock hand is doing a pretty good job. I thought you should know," he told Bud.

"Yeah, I wasn't all that sure about hiring a woman. I don't know where she's from. Her English isn't great. I gave her a chance to prove herself. She does the job of two, and I only have to pay for one." Bud laughed and headed off to the blockhouse. The tightwad took the extra beer with him.

"Are we going back out again, Nash?" Maddie asked.

"I think I'd like to see what shows up instead. If Bud is making enough to survive, I want to see it for myself. We need to know what we're up against."

Over the course of a couple of hours, he counted at least a dozen empty boats fueling and resupplying before heading back to Bimini. he didn't hear Luz ask questions. She appeared to nod and smile a lot and pocket tips. He didn't ask, either, although he helped her out with the fuel lines a couple of times.

The captains didn't waste time ashore. While they were being refueled, they made their way to the shack where they paid cash for the fuel and food and water to tide them over the 50 or 60 mile return trip. He was pretty sure they were handing off more than that to Bud, but he'd need to see it for himself to be certain.

He knew from Luz's Bimini exploration they would do the same thing all over again the next night in a never-ending cycle. Bud had to be raking it in hand over fist for his services—whoever and whatever they included.

Chapter 17

Jim and Maddie were exhausted from the efforts of the night before. Worry about dodging unlit boats, refugee smuggling, maybe even drug smuggling, was heavy on their minds.

The broken air conditioner in the Largo Motel room didn't help. Neither of them could sleep on sweaty sheets. They ended up talking through what they witnessed. Even more important, they talked about what might have happened with the people transported ashore once they climbed into that van.

Jim wasn't happy in the least seeing them herded like that. He tried to justify it by telling himself it was why they were getting paid the big bucks. They needed to follow one of those vans to see where it ended up and what became of the people in it. That became the goal, and he discussed it with Maddie.

"There's three of us, Nash. We can only do so much," Maddie said. "I suppose I could wait in the parking lot for you to conclude another trip tonight.

If I don't go out on the boat, Bud will get suspicious if I suddenly tear out of the parking lot."

Luz wouldn't be able to do it. She had a job on the wharf that allowed her to get to know the smugglers and who they were. She couldn't desert that. It had to be Maddie.

"What kind of setup do you think they could have? One building to hold all of them? More than that? Do you think they hold them like prisoners until they can be sold?" He didn't want to think about that part of it. It was too depressing. "We're a part of the problem now. We're doing the dirty work. I wonder what Bud's going rate is? Did he tip his hand when you were tipping his beer back?"

"He told me he'd never seen our boat before. So I guess we were an unknown. I think he took us for a couple of tourists wanting to fish. When we returned with that load, his eyes were wide enough."

"I wonder if we should think about docking a little farther north. What do you think?" He looked across at Maddie in the dark room.

"I don't think it will matter. It wouldn't surprise me to find out all the small marinas are in on it. All they want is to cash in on a problem that no one can solve."

He was pretty sure Maddie was right. "Pull the charts and we'll have a look. We have to be sure to tell Luz. When we don't show up, she'll be worried." He was sure about one thing. He didn't want to get on the wrong side of Luz. They needed her. She was essential to this operation.

"Maybe you should check in with Emma tomorrow. She must have had a look at her bank account by now to see if we meant business." Maddie had transferred the money as soon as it landed in the business account. It couldn't hurt to check.

He didn't know how to take the illegality of what they were doing with the human trafficking. On the one hand, it went against everything he and Maddie stood for. Luz, too, with her background. How could they possibly justify smuggling people into the country, people that they knew were going to be shipped off to do who knows what?

They couldn't.

The sooner they were done with this operation, the better, as far as he was concerned. Washing the stink off would be another matter.

"We need to get together with Luz to work out how we're going to follow one of those vans," Jim said. "Do you think you could work the wharf if she doesn't show for a night?"

"It would only be part-time, right? I have no clue where fuel tanks or anything else are on those boats."

Maddie was right. Bud probably wouldn't be happy. He might even think something was up.

"I'll do my best, but if I have to fight off Bud's wandering hands, you're in trouble, Nash."

Chapter 18

They were settling into the nightly routine of ferrying people into the country. It didn't take much with the never-ending parade of supply-boats to deliver them. Three nights of an almost full moon helped them feel safe at sea. Jim didn't care to think what kind of screw-up it would be during a cloudy night, or a no-moon situation. The blackness would have to be overwhelming for the faint of heart, meaning them.

Running without lights seemed to be problem enough for them, given the half-assed radar they had. It would only paint something when they were on top of a swell. Still, it was better than nothing. Barely. If the target was an oil tanker. Or a container ship.

Maddie ended up filling in for Luz when she called in sick with female problems. Bud wanted nothing to do with that, as Luz correctly surmised. The excuse freed her to chase after the vans as they came and went from the wharf. On a busy night, she had her pick.

When Luz texted, Jim headed off to meet her at an abandoned warehouse north of Largo Palms. It was dark, with no lights beyond the moon. She scouted the place and determined there were no lights or cameras as far as she could tell. "They head into the south end of the city. It appears as though there are storage areas giving them access with no questions asked. Where they go from there is another problem."

It wouldn't be theirs. Once they notified the feds where the pipeline ended, it was up to them to track the people and their dispersal from there. He didn't want to think where all the people arriving by boat went, or what they ended up doing. The feds had to be desperate if they needed to bring them into it. He wondered how many other small private agencies were involved. Surely theirs couldn't be the only one.

He couldn't ask Evie. She stayed away. Either she knew better, or was under orders. That was fine with him. They didn't need more complications than they had.

It wasn't that complicated, though. It was actually straightforward. With Maddie as the dock hand, he headed out with running lights until he was out of sight of shore, where he switched them off and ran blind under the moonlight. The meet-ups went smoothly once he placed all the coordinates into the nav system. Then it became a matter of meeting the boats, loading up, and heading back to shore.

He wondered why there were no Coast Guard patrols over the open water. After a couple of nights, he stopped wondering. It wasn't his job. He dedicated himself to one thing only, and that was moving people. It went fast in the over-powered panga.

Once he got the routine down, he was doing two, sometimes three, trips a night.

Bud was happy.

He was happy.

As for Maddie, she was a lot happier when Luz came back to work.

Luz briefed us on what she learned of the pipeline into the city. It wasn't good.

Following her first foray chasing after a van, she did three more sorties. The conditions in the storage units were horrible. Buckets and fresh water were at a premium. Many of the refugees—because that's what they were—were weak. Some were sick. There were no doctors. No medical supplies. Nothing beyond a bit of food.

All that didn't make any of them feel better. It was time to take matters into their own hands. After discussing it with Maddie and Luz, they agreed. There was one problem, though. Agreeing was fine. Doing something about the magnitude of the problem was something else.

He set up a meeting with Luz at the abandoned warehouse for the next day. We hit a rib shack for takeout before heading to the meeting with Luz. Maddie busied herself bouncing ideas off him as they completed the short drive.

"Is there any way we can involve Emma in this? A 911 call for one of those human warehouses should do something, wouldn't you think? Wouldn't the techs have to report what they found when they got there?"

He had to admit it was worth a try. "Let's talk to Emma and see what she thinks."

And that's exactly what they did.

Maddie hung up the phone and joined Luz and Jim as they devoured the ribs. "Holy crap, you two. Did you leave any for me?" She stood back with her hands on her hips as they cast innocent looks her way.

"You were busy. What did Emma say?"

Like he couldn't tell from overhearing Maddie's excitement during her phone conversation. Emma's fervor had fairly traveled over the cellphone void to be amplified by that of Maddie. He already figured she agreed.

He passed his ribs off, and they were forced to wait until Maddie finished. He was sure the act was on purpose, but who was he to judge?

"Those ribs are pretty good. We should go there for a sit-down celebration when we finish with this operation," she said.

Maddie chugged her beer and belched and Luz giggled and he thought he might be in the company of a couple of teenagers. He rolled his eyes in jest.

Chapter 19

Maddie's excitement at the prospect of involving Emma in our case was palpable. "She says thanks, Nash. You know what for. She's eager to help us, but her current station isn't anywhere close to any of the warehouses. She'll need a bit of time to work something out. A shift change or something. She'll make some phone calls and let us know."

That was good enough for him. Emma always came through, no matter what he asked of her.

"There's one more thing," Maddie said.

Oh-oh. There was always something when Maddie and Emma got talking. This time, it was a phone call. In person could be worse.

"Luz, Emma wanted to know if you'd like her for a neighbor."

Luz didn't have to think about that. "A neighbor? There are no vacant suites in my block. I don't think she could afford it."

Luz hesitated for only a split second before going

on. "How does she know where I live?"

There was more than a little suspicion in that question. It definitely wasn't good, coming from Luz that way. He knew Luz was fairly comfortable. Her previous occupation as a well-respected Mexican sicario had done her well—not that he was willing to admit to a soul that he knew anything about it.

"No, no, Luz. We have an empty place in our block," Maddie explained." Someone graduated college and moved out to take her first permanent job. It would be you who would move."

From the look on Luz's face, he knew she never for a minute contemplated doing anything like that. He was pretty certain she wanted all the privacy she could get. In fact, he suspected she might move every six months or so, to protect her anonymity.

"I will think about it." It was all she said.

That was a new one. His jaw almost bounced off the wharf. He thought he covered for it when he asked how they were doing with relocating the refugees. The women hemmed and hawed and ignored me. Just as he suspected.

"Need I remind anyone that we need to stop providing women to these losers? We should be rounding up the perps."

The women had their backs to Bud's blockhouse. He had a clear view of the place. Bud was climbing up on a stepladder. A simple light bulb, he figured. Then my own light bulb went off. He was stashing something in the ceiling. He didn't need a university degree to figure out what. He didn't say anything about it to the women.

"Maybe the three of us could get together at the

motel. What do you think?" he asked.

It was a long shot, especially with Luz on the outside and not part of our boat crew. She was the lowly dock hand, not some boat owner eager to earn a little extra cash.

"I will try. Do not be surprised how I show up."

That was good enough for me. Maddie looked more than unsure. He knew better than to question Luz about things like that, especially considering our recent Mexico search and destroy.

They kept the room lights off. Maddie's pacing was driving him crazy. Not only was it a small room, but the floor creaked with every step she took. He wanted to tell her to take it outside. "Will you relax? If Luz can, she'll be here. If she can't—"

The door behind Maddie opened silently, allowing light from the parking lot to spill into the dark room.

"Finally. Maddie was driving me crazy with her impatience."

Luz dropped a pizza box on the table. "I have a part-time job. You will dig in before I have to go."

The woman and her ingenuity never ceased to amaze him.

"We haven't heard from Emma. We're not going to wait. We need to put a stop to Bud's nighttime activities. He's moving dozens of women from our boat alone."

Luz interrupted. "Yes he is. There's no telling what he's doing when I am off in the van delivering women. If he gets more, I cannot say."

"Let's say he is. What do you think we should do?" he asked.

"Have you heard from Evie?"

Evie was the one person he hadn't heard from. If she was heading up this fiasco, she wasn't doing an outstanding job of it beyond the kidnapping attempt on me she had flubbed.

"Bud isn't going away. I think we can depend on him to be a constant. He's too greedy to halt his activities on his own. Let's hope the local authorities will take care of him." He went on. "We need you on the wharf, Luz. You're the only one we can trust with the women we bring ashore."

Maddie's phone rang. She held up her hand for silence. She mostly listened, and when she hung up, she was grinning like a banshee. "That was Emma."

He was beginning to think Emma was avoiding them since they had asked her for help. "Some good news, I hope."

Maddie went on to fill them in.

"Yes. She was able to convince an ambulance crew to visit the holding area I told her about. The crew convinced the guards that someone had called in a pregnant woman in the midst of giving birth. Once they got inside, they called 9-1-1 and SWAT descended."

All three practically jumped for joy, relieved to hear the news.

"Yup. She says the place has been secured, and the guards arrested. Immigration is working overtime as we speak."

Good news, but it didn't solve the problem. They were still in the middle of it, right at the source. They had been transferring boatloads of immigrants non-stop. They all ended up delivered to the human warehouses. That one had been shut down only meant that another would replace it. Probably within hours.

They were pissing into the wind.

Chapter 20

They were failing. Perhaps not in the truest sense of the word, but they were definitely flailing. There was nothing they could do about it. "I understand now how ineffective the Coast Guard was with the Bimini smugglers, Luz. It's like they were trying to plug a sieve. After seeing it first hand, it really is like that. It's unbelievable. It can't be done."

Maddie nodded. "I feel like they knew that when they hired us. If that's the case, why?"

She was right, of course, but there was nothing they could do beyond what they already had. "We're here now, and our first ten days will be up tomorrow. If we don't get another fifty thousand, we're out of here. As fast as we can scramble. In fact, if another fifty lands, I'm for pulling the plug. We'll head home and write the report. What do you two say?"

It was only fair to ask. Both were putting in the work. Did they want to piss into the wind with me?

He was concerned about Luz. He knew she didn't like to surrender. The good thing was that we wouldn't have to wait for a check to clear. It would be a direct deposit.

Luz said, "No, you are right, James. The fight is useless. Nothing will halt the smuggling pipeline. People. Drugs. Weapons. There is no change. What is the point of going on?"

Luz was obviously disappointed. They all were.

"What I'd like to know is, why did they choose me? Us? Was it on Evie's recommendation? How did she even know where I was?"

Then it occurred to him. "Diana."

He couldn't prevent the name from passing his lips. Diana knew where he was, only too well. Maddie perked up instantly before he could bite his own tongue. He was in for it. Maddie was too familiar with the woman's wiles when it came to him, and he didn't want to be reminded.

"What the hell would she want with us now? With you, now? I thought that was settled. It has been, right, Nash?"

Luz didn't know what to make of what she was hearing, and he didn't want to talk about it, especially with Maddie in front of him.

"Diana is an old flame from my, uhh, how should I put it?"

Maddie knew how to put it. "She's an ex fed who almost got Jim killed on my watch, Luz. If she has anything to do with this, I'll kill her myself, and Jim knows it. Diana knows it, too."

Luz knew when enough was enough. She held up her hands. "I'll let you two work it out. It's not my business. I have pizza to deliver to the wharf."

She laughed and headed off on her bicycle. It couldn't have been more than a couple of minutes when my phone rang. It was Luz to announce we had company. "Call if you need my services."

I flipped off the lights before hanging up.

"What's going on, Nash?"

"That was Luz. She says there's someone monitoring us."

They went through their weapons routine. They slipped magazines and smacked them into place. There were boxes for spare ammunition. The extra magazines were in place, where they needed them if they had to get to them quickly.

"We're good to go. We can't do more. Let's get some sleep. Tonight is coming up faster than we want it to," he said.

They had no idea what they were going to do about the situation with the refugees they were bringing ashore. Sure, they wanted the fed money. Sure, they thought they could handle the assignment. But could they? Not even the Coast Guard could do due diligence. How could they be expected to? They had nowhere near the resources the Coast Guard had available.

"There is no way we can make even a dent in those boats and their occupants," he said. "I feel like we're paddling uphill against Niagara Falls."

They climbed into bed.

Maddie snuggled up to him. "Nice pillow talk, Nash." She threw off the covers and sat up. "This is going to be our last night. Get dressed. I know where Bud lives. We need to scout him out."

He had a sneaking suspicion Maddie spent far too much time drinking beer with the man, but who was he to disagree? He climbed out of bed and joined her. They pulled on tourist clothes. They crossed the street to be greeted by the rising sun over the ocean. It looked to be another fantastic day if they were tourists. The problem with that was, they weren't.

"You're kicking yourself for being talked into this deal, aren't you?" Maddie asked.

It was true. He had eyes on the money. Once the feds agreed to pay, he was a hundred percent sold on the deal. "We're still going to get our second payment. I guarantee it, Mads."

Maddie slipped around the rear of Bud's place while he settled in at the locked front door. It swung open, and Maddie greeted me. "Nobody home. We're searching the place while we can."

We tossed the obvious places, on the lookout for documents, cash, badges, anything that would reveal something about Bud.

"He must keep everything in the blockhouse at the wharf. There's nothing here," Maddie said. She was disappointed.

He was, too. "That makes sense. He's almost always there. He can keep an eye on everything." They had nothing. Not a damned thing. "We might as well go back to bed, girl. We got nuttin'."

Maddie winced at my expression.

"So now you're my grammar police?" She grabbed my hand and pulled me across the street to our room. We stripped off and made for the bed. I cranked up the window-shaker on the way.

There was no sense taking any chances.

Chapter 21

They found themselves at an impasse. Jim had hoped they would be able to make a dent in human trafficking operations. They all had. It was impossible. He should have picked up on it from Luz's Bimini briefing and what she witnessed. Instead, pig-headed as he was, he went forward with it. It turned out to be a waste of everyone's time.

So be it. He was ready to give it up and take what he could from it. They didn't need the go-fast any longer. "Luz can blow the boat."

Maddie looked at him incredulously. "She can? How—"

"Don't ask." He changed the subject. "We need to get to Bud and find out what he knows about other marinas up and down the keys that are doing what he's doing. He seems to know more than he lets on."

"You're right," Maddie said. "In between grabbing my ass, he likes to tell tall tales about how much he knows. I chalked it up to hard-on university."

He had to ask, even though he knew he probably shouldn't. "Hard-on university?"

Maddie was grinning. "Yeah. You never heard of it?"

Jim shook his head, knowing something was coming his way.

Maddie went on. "It's like when you meet a woman in a bar and start telling her tall tales of misadventure, expecting it to get you into bed. You've never done it?"

She had me there. But maybe only a time or dozen. He pretended to think. "Yeah, well—"

"Thought so. Come on. I can't wait to corner Bud."

It was dark when they made it to the wharf. Luz was busy checking fuel and oil levels on a couple of other boats. She nodded as they walked past on their way to the go-fast.

"Check the compartments for our firearms. Just in case."

Maddie bent to the task.

He had no choice but to admire her backside.

"Nash, I'm busy. Stop checking out my ass."

He gave her a swat with the flat of his hand and she got busy rubbing at it. "You bastard. That hurt like the devil."

"Like the devil you are is what you mean. Is everything in place?" I asked. Sometimes, I just couldn't help myself.

Neither could Maddie. "You weren't asking about that last night, sailor."

"Maybe not, but you weren't bent over like that."

She straightened. "We're good to go to repel all boarders."

"Then let's get out there and make some money."

He started the engines and had them idling as Luz untied.

He eased away from the wharf. On reaching the breakwater, he firewalled the throttles, and they were off.

The panga bounced in the light chop the farther they got from shore. The bow slapped the water and powered through thanks to the three engines and the five hundred horsepower associated with them. He planed and the ride smoothed only a bit. He leaned into Maddie and his lips found her ear. "It's going to be a rough night."

"Not a problem. I'll just make a grab for the jackline and lean over."

Maddie had donned a life jacket on the first night. Tonight was no different. Yet again, he demonstrated the strobe, and how to fire it, as well as the inflation cord.

He moved to pull away, and she kissed him on the cheek. He made a grab for her and pinched her ass.

"Sailor, pay attention to duty or I'll have you swabbing the deck."

"That won't be necessary after tonight," he reminded her.

He slowed to meet three inbound boats and offloaded sixteen. The seventeenth was a young girl. She clutched at her pack as though it contained everything she owned in the world. It probably did. She leaned over the gunwale with the pack in front of her. I reached for it. She shook her head, a look of panic on her face.

The boats bounced on the waves and separated.

The girl slipped past the jackline.

Maddie tried to reach her as she went over.

He cut the engines.

The heavy backpack carried the girl beneath the waves. Maddie's fingers closed on nothing. She screamed. "Dammit, Jim. God damn it."

The frustration in her voice was telling. Beneath the full moon, the water foamed. The girl floated to the surface and sputtered and coughed.

"Grab her," he yelled. "Grab her before she sinks again."

He helped Maddie pull the grateful young woman into the boat. She struggled to get a leg over the gunwale. He leaned out to get a grip on her pants and tugged her in. Tears of gratitude slid down her face to mix with the ocean water.

"Let's go, Mads. There's no more room."

The scared and confused looks of our passengers had followed them aboard. Maddie's schoolgirl Spanish seemed to do the trick, and they mostly calmed down for the trip to shore and Bud's wharf. The rescued passenger paid her bill by helping quell the looks of despair on many of the faces.

Luz tied us up.

Bud hurried down to get a head count, not wanting to miss out on his finder's fee.

"Do you have anything this girl can wear? We had to pull her out of the water. She's freezing." The soaking wet young girl shivered between us.

"Not likely. What do you think I am, a babysitter?"

Behind him, unseen, Luz moved to strike.

"No."

Bud didn't realize it. His life had been saved with a single word he thought was a response to his question.

Maddie gestured to her car. "I have some things in a bag. Give us a couple of minutes."

Bud moved to accompany the pair into the darkness beyond the wharf's lights. Maddie turned to address him. "I'll let you know when we're ready to go."

Here was a huge part of their dilemma. They were providing aid and comfort to people who would end up on the short end of things. Prostitutes. Slave or no wage laborers in a kitchen. Drug sellers working for nothing. It was all their fault. There was no justice. No reward. Nothing.

Jim sat down beside Luz. "Is Bud worth anything? Could we get something useful from him?"

"I double it, Santiago. Maybe the locations of a few others doing the same. But, no, I do not think it will be useful for us. I agree with you. We should not have taken on this job. The sooner we leave this place, the better it will be for all of us."

He knew she was right.

Chapter 22

Loud voices announced the return of Maddie and Bud to the fold. Bud was loudly insisting Maddie shouldn't be treating the refugees with any degree of compassion. He was fairly screaming at her. Luz stood up, at the ready.

"No, Luz. Maddie can take care of herself. Perhaps not as well as you—"

Luz sat back down, but she didn't relax. Her body remained tense. Ready for action—whatever action she thought would be required.

"You are right." She didn't offer an apology.

In any case, he didn't expect one would be forthcoming. "We're going to wrap this deal up when we're done tonight, Luz."

She was fed up, too. "In that case I will take the boat out and meet you at the motel if that is fine with you."

He nodded. It wasn't the first time Luz got rid of a boat he had used, and he wondered how many she had put out of their misery since?

"We'll scrub this place clean. It shouldn't take long." He didn't make any suggestions. Luz knew what had to be done. Immediately, Luz stood up and made for the fuel dispenser. She flipped the handle, and it powered up with a dull hum. She walked down the wharf to the nozzle.

Jim helped her tug the hose to the very end.

Maddie and Bud were visible through the blockhouse window. They were arguing about something, too busy to notice much of anything.

The fuel pump motor groaned from the effort of the long rubber hose. Luz busied herself pouring fuel over everything that floated. For the most part, that was the wooden wharf and anything attached to it. She reached our panga and gave it a wide berth. In the few lights that remained on the dock, a slimy reflection looked back at us.

When Luz reached the blockhouse, she halted. The stink had to be wafting through the open door. Bud exited, sniffing the air as he did. He recognized the smell immediately. "What the hell are you doing?"

A flattened woman's hand found his solar plexus, and he collapsed to the ground. Luz dragged him into the blockhouse and hoisted him into a chair with practiced ease. It appeared as though it wasn't the first time she had done something similar. She withdrew a roll of tape from a bag and taped Bud's wrists to the chair's arms. His ankles ended up taped to the legs.

She tipped the chair back and began dragging chair and man out to the wharf.

"I have some questions. I will be back," she announced.

Maddie appeared concerned. "What's she going to do with him?"

he figured he already knew. "She's working. Don't bother her. You might be sorry."

"In that case, you two can meet me at the car when you've finished with the questions."

Maddie whirled and walked away. Her intonation didn't go unnoticed.

He used the time to join Luz and a subdued Bud on the wharf. "Anything useful?"

She shook her head. "The usual *I didn't know* and *Please don't kill me.*"

"Yeah, I figured that. He's useless. Did you ask him who he was talking to on the landline? I saw him make a call while he was with Maddie."

He turned back to Luz.

Bud's chin was already resting on his chest.

"He has nothing more for us," Luz said. "You must go and join Maddie. I will see you back at the motel after I dispose of the boat."

Luz stepped into the panga and fired it up.

He walked the length of the dock through the fuel.

The throttles advanced.

A flare ignited and arced through the darkness. It landed on the fuel-soaked wharf.

Jim slammed the blockhouse door behind him. The sound wasn't loud enough to disguise the whump of the igniting fuel.

An orange glow shone through the blockhouse window.

Jim climbed up on the desk and reached to move a ceiling panel. A cache of money slipped out and fell to the floor. He poked at a few more tiles and was rewarded again.

He jumped down, found a paper bag, and loaded up.

He figured the cartels would never miss it, given the speed with which the flames were eating their way toward the blockhouse. Already, sirens were growing louder in the distance.

"Go, Maddie."

She opened her mouth to speak.

"No. We don't have time for questions. It's time to go."

Chapter 23

Maddie drove to the motel in complete silence. "We had to do something, Mads. You know it and I know it. Otherwise, it's like we've been treading water."

It was true. She knew it. "It's just so damned frustrating, Jim. We invested time and money in this deal, and it's not worth shit. To anyone."

"You saved that girl's life. That's something," he said.

"Saved her for what? From being a hooker? Whoop-dee-doo and BFD."

He didn't see the sense in arguing. It was obvious to all of them. He slipped the key into the motel room door. Before he could reach for the light switch, a fist slammed into his gut. He doubled over and went down.

Maddie tripped and fell over him on the carpet.

In the light coming through the window, he witnessed a bag pulled over Maddie's head. Another ended up over mine. They were in the shit now. So much for those best laid plans.

Who was onto them? Bud was out of the picture, unless he said something before they neutralized him. Maybe it was the phone call he saw him making. But what did he have to tell anyone? They were meticulous in doing their jobs. No one knew anything.

No one, except for Lucky Lucy. And she had a handler. The handler would know, too.

Engine noise from the back side of the motel filtered through the open room door. It died, and then there was silence.

He knew what was going to happen next. "If you know what's good for you, you'll let us go," he said.

Laughter followed by a couple of random kicks told him their captors weren't going to listen. Why would they? Were he in circumstances similar, he wouldn't listen, either. He'd be doing exactly what they were doing—crowing about how easy it was to capture them.

"There's going to be an explosion on the water. A few minutes after that, someone will come for us. Believe me, you do not want that person to find you here."

More laughter only repeated what he feared would be true. It would be a massacre of their own making. Still, Maddie doubted him, too.

"Do you really think she'll come for us? She has no idea we've been captured."

"The good part about all this is that we agreed to meet up after she destroyed the panga. You can depend on Luz to keep her word."

The only question was, how many bodies would pile up while Luz was keeping it?

He had part of an answer when an explosion rocked the motel to its core. The sky turned orange and the entire building shook. Either Luz had miscalculated, or she was putting on a show.

No one in the room seemed concerned. There was no yelling. No loud voices that said panic.

He tried to sound the minutes. It was impossible. He thought he heard a firearm of sorts, but the sound was muffled. Then he remembered. Luz used a .22 Long Rifle whenever she could.

He announced to the attackers. "Lobo is coming."

There were whispers back and forth. No one made a move. They didn't even close the open door. Instead, a lone voice said everything.

"Lobo is dead."

Those three words were the last until Jim sensed someone step over him and advance into the room.

Luz's handgun spoke twice. Then four more times in rapid succession.

It would seem Lobo wasn't dead after all.

"We need to go, Santiago."

Luz pulled off Maddie's hood and then released mine.

"Gather all the firearms you can," she said. "We are going to have a fight on our hands."

He tossed the mattress and retrieved the two HKs and the matching rails. His Model 17 and its magazines ended up in one of the discarded hoods. He took the time to collect the weapons from the bad guys. When he finished, he had time to ask the question.

"How many, and who?"

Luz was gone. He looked into the parking lot. She was busy cleaning out our car. In the distance, tires squealed and engines roared.

"I cannot say for sure. I only know that someone recognized you from your time in Mexico."

"Our last trip?"

"No. The one before that," she said.

That threw me. I had to stop and think. "You mean—"

"Yes. We have to go. Now."

He grabbed Maddie and pulled her from the room. We hurried to make our way around the back to the two palm trees he recalled from the last fishing trip. He and Don Boyle had a nice setup with a cooler and two lounge chairs and Lola to break the monotony. This time, there would be no monotony.

Already Luz had assessed the situation. "We won't be able to move from here. The boat is finished. It is purely a defensive position."

Tires scraped on the motel's gravel parking lot. Our time was up. Maddie's breathing was fast. Too fast. "Slow down, Mads. We have plenty of ammunition."

"It's not that, Nash. How the hell are we going to get out of here when it runs low?" she asked.

He looked across at Luz in the dark.

She could only shrug.

He was sure she thought a response wasn't required.

He had one trick left up his sleeve.

"Give me your phone."

Chapter 24

More cars skidded into the parking lot, kicking up more dust and gravel. Doors slammed. Voices cursed over the noise.

"Somebody doesn't sound happy to be here."

It was as though they already knew they were about to be in a battle royal, and he wondered who or what had clued them in. Whatever it was, it was some small comfort to have Luz with them.

"I think they know I am back, Santiago. But that is not so much. They know you are here with me."

How could he forget? For more than a few of the cartels, he was KOS—kill on sight. He was pretty sure Luz was on that list, too. He told her so.

She only shrugged. "Yes. So? Together we will force them to regret putting us on their lists."

Maddie made a grab for both our hands and pulled us down and out of sight.

Given what was going on, he forgot she was here.

"All right, you two," she said. "The time for

reminiscing about old times is over. We need to move a couple of those palm tree sections behind us."

She was right. Someone had cut up an old tree. It was huge. We grunted and groaned and finally rolled two of the thick sections into place.

"That will stop anything but an RPG. Speaking of which—" He looked at Luz in the dark.

"No. I do not have one of those." She smiled back at me.

The shouting and cursing halted. Silence greeted us from across the lawn.

"They're ready. It should start just about—"

Heavy fire thumped into the palm trees. Cool as a cucumber, Luz returned fire with the suppressed HK toward the muzzle flashes. She found the mark, and more than a few groans accompanied her aim into the dark.

"They are setting us up for some of them to work their way behind us. I will come back." Luz disappeared into the dark.

He and Maddie stopped their shaking. They were returning fire, although at a somewhat slower rate than they were taking it. They needed to conserve ammunition. They had to hold out as long as they could."

A sudden lull in the return fire allowed them to reload empty magazines.

"Jim. What's that sound behind us? Are they—"

He had already heard. He recognized it for what it was. "It's Luz. She's taking care of business."

Maddie appeared visibly relieved.

Jim said, "From what I can tell, she should be back any minute. Don't shoot her."

He got a dirty look for his warning as Luz climbed over the jury-rigged backstop. She reloaded her .22 and tucked it into her belt. A second small caliber weapon of the same make hung in a shoulder holster.

"How was it back there?" he asked.

"Not so bad. They are very sloppy."

He didn't need to ask. He was familiar with Luz's abilities.

"How is your ammunition holding out?"

Luz placed three automatics on the ground in front of her. "Not so good. That is all I could collect."

"Our HK is down to half a rail. Maddie and I have a magazine each for our automatic. You?"

"My small caliber weapons are excellent for close in. Not so good for distance. I have one magazine for mine."

He checked the time on the phone. Forty-five minutes. He wasn't so optimistic any more. He dulled the display and pocketed the phone. "We're going to have to wait them out any way we can."

Luz was gung-ho to climb back over the barricade at our rear.

He knew she was all-in for action, but he didn't want her going off on her own. She had already taken care of their rear position.

He reached for the phone and checked the time again. Maddie caught him out.

"Are you heading off to a meeting, or what?" she asked.

"I don't want to take a chance on any of us getting separated." He realized that didn't make any sense.

"There's something I haven't told you."

Chapter 25

Emma opened the office gun safe.

She retrieved handguns. Ammunition. The last remaining HK and two rails. She picked 10K out of the black bag for traveling money and secured the safe. *Traveling money*. It was an expression she wondered about when she heard Jim use it for the first time. She thought it went well with what she was doing.

She loaded the weapons and the cash into the old Packard's concealed storage. She silently thanked Jim for his presence of mind. She thought back to the first time she saw the old car. She thought it was junk, or perhaps something Jim would work on to restore.

She recalled thinking it was a bit of a wreck. He was smart, though. It was a lot heavier, but the souped-up engine and the modern hydraulic brakes more than made up for the weight. Jim had let her drive it a time or two for the fun of it. She knew enough to hit the gas pedal for *go* and the brakes for *stop.*

And that's what she was about to do, until the burn phone rang. She knew who it was without looking. She was expecting to hear how the operation was proceeding. Instead, she was forced to listen to Jim through a hail of gunfire.

She twisted the steering wheel. Immediately, she over-steered with the super-sensitive power steering. At the same time, she tromped on *go*. The Packard lurched into the street. Behind her, horns honked and tires screeched.

She never looked back. She didn't have time. She was busy consulting her phone for location and distance.

Don Boyle spotted the familiar car as he was heading back to the precinct in his city ride. He figured it was Jim, so he tucked in behind it. He intended to pull him over for a quick coffee.

He paced the car to the freeway, where it accelerated, and he lost it. He caught sight of it again and he thought he recognized Emma and the big black dog in the front seat.

Emma floored the Packard. The wind whistled around the convertible's top. Friday squatted beside her on the front seat. He nosed her neck with a cold, damp nose.

"You better jump in the back, dog. You'll be good there if we blow a tire."

The dog obeyed Emma instantly and barked

when he got settled in. For good measure, he sat up and nosed the back of her neck with his cold nose.

"Floor, Friday. On the floor."

The dog whined and woofed to complain, but he obeyed.

Boyle witnessed the dog jumping over the seat and into the back, where he disappeared. "Now where are those two going? It can't be grocery shopping, not at that speed and this time of night."

He was too far from anywhere to swap the city ride with his own car. Emma would be long gone. He cursed Nash silently and wondered what trouble the man was into with the rest of them.

Emma checked her phone. She was making good time on her way to Largo Palms. She cursed when the blues flashed behind her in the mirror. The siren whooped. She mushed the heavy Packard to a stop by the side of the freeway. She wiped sweaty palms on her pants and put them back on the steering wheel.

"Dammit Friday, now we're going to get a ticket."

Friday woofed and jumped up on the back seat. His head went out the open window. He sniffed to test the air. He recognized the scent immediately. His nose found Emma's ear, and he began whining.

"Now what? What is it? Do you need to go potty?"

The big black Lab ignored her and paced back and forth on the back seat. His tail whipped up a storm. Emma hit the button to lower her window.

She took her hands off the steering wheel, intending to reach for her license and the car's registration. At the last minute, she thought better of it.

"Where are you off to, miss? The last time I saw you and Friday alone in a vehicle, you were setting fire to it, if I'm not mistaken."

Emma almost cried out when she recognized the voice. Boyle reached in to pat Friday. The dog quieted immediately.

"Oh. Don. Am I glad to see you. We're on our way to pick up Jim and Maddie and Luz in Largo Palms. I heard gunfire on the phone when they called and and—" Emma gulped.

Already she knew she was talking too much. Jim would kill her when he found out. She knew Don would be sorely tempted to ask for more information. Jim was his friend, after all. They shared a fishing adventure or two. On a couple of occasions, they even stooped to bring home frozen grocery store fish.

"Say no more. I'll take you to the city limits. You're on your own from there."

Emma tucked the Packard in behind Don's city ride, and the two-vehicle convoy high-tailed it to the city's southern limit in jig time. Don signaled and pulled the car to the side of the road. Emma honked the horn and waved as she sped past.

Early morning traffic on the dark sea-to-sky highway was light. It was too early for tourists to be out. The police were nowhere to be found. Her surroundings started to look familiar. She checked her mapping program. It told her she was five minutes away from the Largo Motel.

She reached for the burn phone. Flipped it open. Reconsidered. At the speed she was traveling in the unfamiliar car, her attention was best devoted to driving. She dropped the phone on the seat and checked her own phone's mapping page. The Largo Motel turnoff announced itself in a calm female voice.

She hit the brakes hard. In the back, Friday slid and bumped against the seat. He barked his consternation.

"Sorry Friday. I'll try harder next time. Floor. Stay."

She cranked the wheel to the left. The Packard's front tires squealed and fought her control. The back end swayed but stayed glued to the asphalt.

"Thank goodness for the armor plate in this tank. I don't think it would have stuck without the weight. Right, Friday?"

She floored the accelerator.

Friday barked.

She commanded him a second time. "Floor. Stay."

The Largo Motel's small neon sign poked its way through the stunted palm trees in the front. She braked hard and cranked the steering to the right. The Packard skidded onto the motel's gravel lot. The back end swung out. Emma counter-steered and straightened the Packard on the grass behind the motel.

"We're here, Friday," she announced.

Gunfire erupted all around her. Emma was too busy wrestling with the heavy car to notice.

<h1 style="text-align:center">Chapter 26</h1>

Jim opened his burner to check the time. He cupped a hand to conceal the light, like a soldier in wartime.

"Nash. What the hell? Are you late for a breakfast meeting?" Maddie asked.

A huge orange ball was rising over the ocean to the east. A breeze rustled palm leaves above them.

"Nah. Just checking to see if—"

Tires screamed on asphalt. A car skidded into the motel's unpaved parking lot. Wheels locked and the car kicked up an enormous dust cloud, obscuring the car. Three heads peeked around the palm trunk shelter.

"What the hell is that, Nash? Did our friends call in the cavalry?"

The car hesitated, as though getting its bearings. The engine roared. Spinning tires kicked up gravel. It scattered and ricocheted off the motel's tin siding. The front of the car penetrated the cloud of dust, followed by the rest of it as it launched across the grass toward the palm trees.

"Ladies, it's not a limousine, but our ride-share is here."

"Nash! That's Emma. Nash. Emma. Emma." Maddie stuttered.

Renewed gunfire erupted. Emma's body slipped down in the seat and disappeared. Only her eyes remained to peek between the dash and the steering wheel. The car kept on toward the grove of palm trees.

"Damn it," Jim said. "That woman kept the top up. It's going to get shot up. It'll cost me a fortune to replace."

Maddie's eyes went wide. "She's not going to stop, Jim. Jim—"

The Packard slid sideways in front of the palm trees, providing a barrier against the hail of lead aimed in the group's direction.

Friday barked.

"What is that dog doing here? I thought we left him with Dr. Hannah." Maddie was near panic on hearing her dog.

The car skidded to a stop on the grass. Emma opened the heavy door at the same instant. Unable to control it, the door smashed into a palm tree and stayed open. Friday jumped out.

Emma called to him. Her voice was stern. "Friday. Car. Now."

He turned and barked and obeyed, slowly but surely, reluctant to desert his mistress and her friends. It was his duty to greet everyone to let them know who was here to help.

Upset, Maddie called to him. "Friday. Car. Floor."

The big dog hung his head and remained in the car.

Jim didn't care about that. "Did you bring—" he began.

"Yup. The usual places," Emma replied.

Protected by the armor-plated car, Jim made for each of the compartments. Lead continued to fly in the car's direction. He freed an MP5 rail and passed it to Luz. He clicked the second rail into the HK and handed it off to Maddie. The pistols and the remaining handgun magazines ended up in the Packard's back seat.

Lead pinged off the car's armor plating. The rate of fire raining down on them increased as annoyed and pissed off shooters tried to take them out all at once.

"I wonder how long it will take them to figure out they're aiming at a tank?"

Jim barked orders like a marine in a free-fire zone. "Emma. Get in the back. Luz. Slide into the front. Maddie, in the back with your dog. Any questions? No? Good. Let's blow this pop stand."

A mad scramble ensued as they all slipped into their assigned seats.

Jim got into the empty driver's seat, cranked the wheel, and floored the gas pedal. The Packard came to life immediately. The momentum freed the door from the palm tree. It slammed shut. He cursed and hit the button to put the roof down.

Gunfire halted at the circus as the convertible's top lowered and stowed.

"You didn't think I was serious, did you? What do you think I am, made of money?" He laughed maniacally and aimed the car straight at their attackers. "Bombs away, boys and girls. Fire at will."

Return fire peppered the attackers as they were forced to back against the motel. The car screamed past the end of the motel, out of sight of their attackers. Their firing halted. Luz commanded Jim to halt. He stomped hard on the brake. The motion kicked up a cloud of dust and gravel.

"Wait for me, Santiago. I will be back." Luz forced open the heavy door. Already she was drawing her twin Model 71s.

In the back, Maddie and Emma weren't happy. "Jim? Why are we stopping? What's she doing? Where the hell is she going?"

Maddie, intent on getting out, forced the seat forward. Friday, sensing trouble, was right behind her, ready to follow his mistress where he sensed he was needed.

"Maddie. Stay here. You are definitely not needed."

She wasn't about to listen. She didn't stop for even a second. Jim hooked his hand through her belt and hauled her back. Her feet kicked at empty air.

"Listen to me. You're not needed."

The sound of subdued gunfire from around the back of the motel made its way to the Packard. Two shots. Two more. And two more followed by two more.

"What's she doing? What's that gunfire? It doesn't sound like—"

More sounds of twin rounds being fired made

their way to the car.

Jim turned to Maddie and Emma in the back. "She's cleaning up. She doesn't need you. She doesn't need me. She doesn't need anyone. You do not want to be there. No matter what."

"But she but she—" Emma exclaimed.

"Maddie. Emma. Listen to me. I told you to leave it. Okay? Just leave it."

Luz made her way around the corner and back to the car. She replaced the magazines before getting in. She pulled the heavy door closed and slammed it.

"Bueno, Santiago. Ve ahora. Go now."

Jim nodded tersely and tromped on the accelerator. He skidded the car past the end of the motel and made for the highway.

Luz turned to Emma and Maddie. "Is everyone all right? Is anyone hit? Is Friday all right?"

Friday recognized his name immediately and barked.

It took Emma slightly longer to register the question. Finally, her adrenalin-packed voice screamed from the back. "Does anyone mind if I scrape out my pants right here?"

Luz giggled. "Emma. Thank you for coming to help us. You did a good job. We thought Jim kept checking the clock because he was counting the hours until we would be out of ammunition and they would storm our barricades."

Jim joked to ease the tension. "I don't want rumors circulating that we don't take care of our girls. Right, Friday?"

That was Friday's cue. He barked once and jumped up on the back seat. He scrambled across

Maddie's lap and stuck his nose against Jim's neck.

"Zelda. Bad dog."

Friday did it again, because he always did after the man called out Zelda's name.

Maddie wasn't so happy. "Why did you bring Friday, Emma? I thought we left her with Dr. Hannah."

Maddie's tone was enough for Emma to know the woman wasn't happy she brought her dog into a free-fire zone.

"I picked him up at the kennel when I didn't hear from you guys. I thought he'd be happier with me until you came home." She hesitated. "I didn't know I'd be taking an armored car and a dog into a war zone. Had I known—"

Emma halted, knowing when to quit.

Luz chose that moment to interrupt, sensing Emma's discomfort with Maddie.

"We need to get rid of these weapons. All of them. Before we get off this road."

Chapter 27

Don Boyle listened to the report coming over the wire about the shootout in Largo Palms. It was the fishing haunt he shared with Jim Nash. He flipped on the flashing blues and made his way to a familiar intersection. If he was lucky, it would be key in intercepting Nash's return to the city.

He tucked his city ride into a gas station's small parking lot and backed in. The position was ideal to monitor the route he suspected Nash and company would use to get back into the city.

He considered what he'd heard on the wire report. It wouldn't cover everything. How could it? No one knew Jim might very well be the guilty party. No one knew who was there, but for Nash and Emma, judging by the speed with which he helped her vacate the city in Nash's old Packard.

He worried Luz might be involved, too. Ever since Nancy and Jim crossed into Mexico to return the woman home where she belonged, he had his concerns about the young woman. Jim wasn't beyond hiring Luz as an operator in his small private detective business, but he didn't mind that. He knew Nash would keep an eye on her.

It was the backgrounds of Jim and Luz in Mexico concerned him. He knew little about either of them down there. His wife, Nancy, wasn't talking, but that was all right. His wife deserved her privacy, too, when it came to certain things in her background that he wasn't privy to.

The Packard appeared suddenly and screeched to a halt in plain sight at a light across from the gas station. Boyle waited for the light to change before picking up the car. He followed it through lights for a mile or so and then hit the lights and siren.

The car signaled immediately and pulled over. He approached the driver's side door and looked in. Friday stuck his head out the open back window and woofed a greeting. He reached to scratch the dog's ears and received a tail wagging and a doggie smile like no other.

"Hello Maddie. Hello Jim. What's new? How has Friday been? Lola misses seeing you all. Where have you been? Off taking a little vacay from the bright lights and big city?"

He knew damned well where they had been. The description of the car had been a part of the wire report. Their route into the city was on back roads as well—as if that didn't tell him something was up.

Don took a step back and surveyed the driver's side of Nash's Packard. He walked around the opposite side and did the same before sticking his head in through Maddie's window.

"Are you guys all right? What's with the duct tape stuck all over your paint job?"

"Oh, that bit of tape?" Maddie got out and slammed the door.

A nervous Friday attempted to chase after her through the open window.

"Friday. Stay."

She smiled up at the much taller Detective Boyle. "Is that an official question, officer?"

Boyle walked back to the opposite side of the car. Maddie chased after him. Torn pieces of duct tape adorned both sides of the Packard. "We're getting the car ready for a new paint scheme."

Boyle reached for a square of tape, picked at a corner, and peeled it back. "Just as I figured." They would have to go some to put one over on him. "I think you're going to need a little body work first. And judging by the air circulating through that convertible top, you'll need to replace it, too. Now get your asses out of here before I call on every cop I know."

Boyle walked back to his police ride, shaking his head. He switched off the flashing blues and thought he saw Maddie and Nash high-five. He remained parked by the side of the street while the Packard pulled into traffic.

"If I know one thing, where there's smoke, there's fire."

He checked traffic before cranking the wheel to return to his gas-station surveillance spot. Sure enough—

He pulled into the street and hit the blues and the siren on the junker in front of him. It pulled over promptly, almost in the same spot as his first stop. He got out and approached the beater.

"Where are you ladies off to today? Oh, hi Emma." He leaned in the window. "Hi Luz. How are both of you?"

He tried suppressing the grin, but he couldn't. He had Emma dead to rights, and she knew it. "What happened to that big black dog I saw you with last night?"

Emma smiled sweetly up through the window. "Big dog? I'm not sure—"

Boyle didn't let up. "And that really nice car you were driving. A Packard, was it? It kind of resembled Jim Nash's car, wouldn't you say?"

"Oh, I don't know—" Emma began.

"Trouble is, I just said hello to Jim and Maddie a few minutes ago. And guess what? There appeared to be a lot of specialized air conditioning in that thing."

"I'm sure I know nothing about that, officer," Emma said.

"You know how I know?" Boyle didn't wait for an answer. He knew one wouldn't be forthcoming. "I peeled back some of that tape and guess what I found? That's right. Bullet holes. You know anything about that, young ladies?"

He walked around the rusted-out beater, checking for those same bullet holes, and found none.

"Nice ride. You're free to go. Oh, and Luz? You're expected for dinner on Sunday. Trish and Lola have been missing you. You're invited too, Emma."

He pivoted and walked back to his car. The grin was even bigger than it was for Nash and company.

"Those sons of guns have done it again."

He didn't venture to guess what they had done, exactly. He had no idea. If he knew one thing, though, the wire report was only the tip of the iceberg where those four were concerned.

Chapter 28

Jim pulled the bullet-riddled Packard into the parking space in front of his office building. An exhausted Maddie and Jim climbed the stairs to their third-floor apartment. Friday traipsed after them, perhaps sensing the disappointment in the pair.

"I wonder whatever possessed Emma to bring Friday along on the rescue mission? She should have known better, Jim. I'm not happy she put him in danger."

"Oh come on. He was in a tank on the floor. What could have gone wrong?"

"Well—"

"Go grab a shower. You'll feel better. In fact, I'll join you."

He filled Friday's water bowl with ice and water. Friday scurried over and lapped it up. Ice cubes pinged against the metal bowl. "Look at that. He's happy to be home, too."

He did the same for Friday's food bowl and placed it on the floor beside the water. The huge dog dug in like it was his first meal in days. Satisfied that his duties were complete, Jim headed off to join Maddie in the shower.

Emma parked the beater behind Jim's car, and she and Luz headed up to her place. On the way, she used a key to let Luz into the empty apartment that had been Anya's. "What do you think?"

Before Luz entered, she gestured down the hall. "That is your place by the window?"

Emma nodded.

Luz went from room to room in Anya's former apartment, assessing everything she felt she needed in order to feel safe. If she took the place, she would talk to Jim about a steel-reinforced door and safer windows and that fire exit staircase hanging off the third-floor end-window. There would be a lot of work needed.

She knew she was being selfish, but she also knew she had to not only be safe, but to feel safe, too. "I will talk to Jim about some changes, but I think I like it. Can I look at yours now?"

The two apartments were twins, laid out almost exactly the same.

"If it is all right with you, I will make some suggestions to Jim about your place as well. I can afford the upgrades if you cannot."

Emma was about to ask the woman what she meant by upgrades, but decided it was for another time. For now, she wanted to get some food, get some rest, and take a shower. "I'll order Chinese for all of us, okay?"

"I cannot. I promised Don I would visit with Tricia and Lola."

Emma knew Nancy and Luz had become close since she came to Florida. She thought there was more between the two women, but she wasn't sure how it went. She thought she saw a familial resemblance between the two women, but she always shrugged it off. It was none of her business.

"If you're tired, you can spend the night here. The sofa unfolds into a bed and I have extra sheets and blankets. I'm sure Don would understand if you called him."

Emma picked up a post-it and a pen. She wrote a note and handed it to Luz. "That's the combination to my gun safe. Can I tell Jim and Maddie you might move in? Would that be all right? I don't want to get in your way."

"You may tell him I looked at the place. I have some concerns I need to discuss before I will move."

She said nothing to Emma about her concerns.

Maddie turned the water off and grabbed a towel. Jim stood back, admiring her glistening body in the light. "Why don't we have a little snooze before we eat? I could use the break."

"If I know you, it's not a snooze you're wanting, Mr. Pervert Detective."

"Look who's detecting now, smarty-pants. Are you going to join me or not? And by the way, that's Private Detective to you."

He pulled back the covers, and Maddie slipped in ahead of him. Friday made to jump up on the bed, a definite no-no that he knew not to do.

"Friday. Time for bed. Go. Now."

Resigned, Friday doggie-sighed and slunk out of the bedroom. His toenails clicked on the floor all the way to his bed in the kitchen. For spite, he barked once before he settled on his bed.

"I guess he just told us."

Maddie snuggled against Jim. "He can tell us all he wants, but I'm the boss and he knows it."

Jim said nothing. For once, he knew when to shut up.

Chapter 29

Last night's pillow-talk with Maddie resolved some misgivings Jim was having regarding the contract with the feds. He said to hell with all of it and submitted another bill for fifty thousand. It was report writing time, and he would not be kind.

He headed for the office and closed and barred the door. Maddie showed up with her key and lunch and then left him in peace to finish up. Everything they did was legal—like he would admit otherwise. he left out the gore and illegal stuff because no one, not even him, could be that dumb.

He wrote up the survey of Bimini to get some idea of the magnitude of the problem. He told them about setting up on Largo Palms with a panga. Told them about the contacts they made. The how and why and the expense list they incurred to get the information.

The largest part of the report covered the clearance centers they located. He detailed locations of the storage centers. He included estimates of numbers of

people processed. There were hundreds, possibly thousands, of illegals being regularly processed through those makeshift facilities.

He covered off the boats launched out of Bimini and the methods used to get the illegals ashore. How none of the boats showed up at a marina with anyone but the captain and a helper. No papers or passports were requested. How they fueled and oiled and departed right away, headed for home to prepare for another load the next night.

He made sure they knew there was no way to stop it. If they had questions about that, they should consult with their own Coast Guard to back him up. Whether that would happen was a story for another day.

He finished by suggesting the only way to cure the Bimini problem was to annex the islands or float a blockade around it.

He wasn't jesting.

At the last minute, he included a paragraph about the boats that never made shore, but refueled on the spot at sea and returned to Bimini. It further made his point.

What anyone could or would or wouldn't do about it wasn't their problem.

He finished and brought it up to Maddie for her input. She corrected sentences and some of the grammar and wrote in her additions. She agreed one hundred percent.

He couldn't go wrong with her help.

"When the next 50K clears our account, they'll get their report," he said.

"They won't be happy, James."

"I wouldn't be either, but like I said, not our problem. It's why I'm waiting on the second 50."

They sighed in unison. "Do you think Lucky Lucy aka Evie will be happy with the results?"

"Who cares? As long as she doesn't darken our doorstep again, I'm happy," he said. "One more thing. I'd like to show this to Luz before I send it in."

Maddie looked at him quizzically.

"I want her to feel she's a part of our operation."

"She's a definite asset. We wouldn't have been able to get as far as we did," Maddie said.

"Good. I'm glad you think that way. Let's do lunch."

Emma and Luz walked into the office.

Friday perked up immediately at the familiar women in his life.

"Lunch? Where are you taking us, Nash? We missed breakfast, in case you didn't notice."

Friday woofed when he realized he missed out on Emma's bacon bits under the table. He perked up when he heard Luz's soothing voice.

"Emma showed me Anya's place last night. I like it. Whoever did the work did an excellent job."

Maddie perked up. She liked Luz, even as she was realizing the woman was a cold-blooded killer. "So does that mean you'll take it?" she asked.

"No. Not right away. I have some things to discuss with the owner and the manager of the building," she said.

Behind his desk, Jim stood up. "That would be me." He was about to sit back down when he realized his mistake. "And Maddie. Maddie is the owner and manager, too."

Luz's gaze shifted to Maddie. "I will get back to you in a day or so if that will be all right." She reached down to pat Friday. "For now, I must go home. I will get ready to visit with Nancy and Don."

Chapter 30

Luz was unsure what to think of the offer to move into the Nash building. While it would certainly provide a permanent home for her—for that's what she considered it to be—she thought it dangerous, considering her background. She was relocating every six months. Still, she was comfortable with that. Her upscale living quarter rentals made sure she went unrecognized by her workmates at the grocery store.

That was another thing. She would have to give up her job if she moved into their building. It wasn't reasonable to expect to commute to what she considered her day job at the supermarket. The job provided her with cover.

Luz got out a pencil and the parchment paper she used for cooking. She tore off a long sheet and sketched out the Nash building. She went online and got the official drawings as well. She wanted all the bases covered, including electric and water and sewer.

Telephone lines, too.

When she finished, she had an excellent picture of what she wanted. Now all she had to do was present it and talk Jim and Maddie into the changes. It would be incumbent on him to arrange for contractors to do the work. She didn't want to have to go through that, given that many of the laborers would be Cuban or Mexican. Jim would have to do the dealing. She would pay, of course. After all, the modifications were at her request.

She put the work aside and got ready to visit with Nancy and Don. She was looking forward to seeing Tricia—her *manita*, she called her—and Lola, too. She loved all four of them dearly. The antics Lola went through to stay close to her never ceased to make her laugh.

She smiled and recalled the fuss Tricia made when she first called her by that nickname. The girl rushed to her mother to ask what it meant. She came back beaming with pride as she explained to Lola—as though the dog would understand that it meant *little sister*. That the dog didn't understand didn't matter to Tricia, though. It made her happy, and that's what did matter.

She would ask for Nancy's opinion on whether to make the move. She valued having Nancy in her life even more after she had accompanied Jim to bring her back from Mexico. She wouldn't mention the changes to the building she wanted Jim to make. That was up to him.

She rode the bus and her bicycle to visit. She enjoyed riding around the city, getting to know it. That she could put her bike on the front of the bus made doing so a lot easier. The residential streets were easy to ride on, unlike the busy downtown area.

On the bike, she kept her eyes wide open, making sure her six was clean. She stopped often to check her reflection. Two side mirrors, plus the one she wore on her helmet, helped. She couldn't be too careful. She was prepared for her past to catch up with her. Nancy's place was where she didn't want it to happen. She would never forgive herself if anything happened to her adopted family.

She considered telling Nancy she thought of them that way, and thought better of it. It wouldn't be fair. Nancy had been more than good to her. Jim, too. But still—

She arrived in time to help set the table while Lola and Tricia fussed around her, pretending to help, but only wanting to be close. She scratched at Lola's ears, and caught herself before brushing at Tricia's hair, too.

When dinner was over, she helped Nancy clean up. Nancy chased Don off to the back yard, out of their way. "Will you be coming over on Sunday? I invited Jim and Maddie and Emma if you're interested. I thought I should warn you, in case it was too many people."

"I will come if I can help to cook for everyone."

Nancy smiled. "You already know I don't turn down help in the kitchen. Should we do a Mexican spread for those freeloaders?"

"I think that would be nice. And Don looks like he needs a bit more in the waist. He appears to be fading away," Luz said. They laughed together until Don came in to see what the fuss was about.

'Did I hear someone mention my waistline? You know, I'm not the only one around these parts with a bit of a muffin top."

Luz held up her hands in surrender. "I don't know what you are talking about. Could it be—"

"That Nash character could stand to lose a few pounds, too. Not to mention that dog of theirs. And if anyone tells Maddie I said her dog was fat—"

"Or her man?" Nancy asked.

"All right, you two. I surrender. Need any help with the dishes?" He looked around the spotless kitchen. "Good. Doesn't look like it. Come on, Lola. Walk time."

He chuckled, hooked up Lola to the leash, and made for the door.

Chapter 31

They all caught up to Luz on the weekend at the Boyle's.

Jim was savvy enough to show up with potato salad fresh from a bulk store. He thought he could pass it off as home made, but smart detective that she was, Maddie pointed out the sticker and the container.

He recognized Tricia's laughing and giggling, and Lola's barking and whining the instant they entered the home. The pair were busy in the back yard doing doggie and girl things.

Soon enough, an anxious Friday and Lola renewed acquaintances.

Tricia glommed onto Maddie until Luz appeared, after which the girl switched her allegiance back and forth for a bit.

Friday didn't know what to do with Luz and Tricia and Lola all in one place. He ran back and forth from the wading pool to douse them all with water from his constant shakes and tail wagging.

Lola joined in the merriment, so there was no rest for the weary.

It was great fun for them until the dogs tired of it. Both ambled off to lie down in the shade tree at the end of the yard. Unfortunately, the break in dog play gave Don a chance to fire off a few questions.

"So, Nash. What have you and your crew been up to lately? I haven't seen hide nor hair of you."

It was only half true, of course. Jim knew he had pulled them over earlier in the week, too.

"Where's your other partner in crime? Is Emma coming over?"

"She's off picking up a new car for herself. She said she'd be here."

"Lucky woman. You didn't answer my question," Nash.

Maddie nudged Jim. She knew he didn't want to get on the wrong side of their good friend. Or his wife. "We took a federal assignment down in Largo Palms for a bit."

"Our fishing spot. I trust you left it in one piece."

Jim looked across at Maddie with a nervous glance.

"Well—"

"Using the masking tape to match your paint job was a nice touch. Whose idea was it?" Boyle asked.

"Anya came up with it on our trip down the Baja a few years ago. I thought it was a great idea."

"Funny how none of that lead went through-and-through, isn't it?"

"Yeah, about that. After that trip down Baja way, I had the Packard armor plated. You know, just in case."

Don looked at Nancy. "Just as I suspected."

Nancy, no fool to her husband's ideas, nodded hurriedly. "Of course, dear. It must have been plain as day."

Jim told Don about Lucky Lucy and their adventure up north, where he thought the woman had been killed. "Turns out she was an undercover fed, of all things. And she lived to tell about it after all these years. I must be getting old. I never spotted it."

Tricia, bored with the turn the conversation had taken, wandered off to sit in the shade with the two dogs. They arranged themselves on either side of her.

"I heard about a firefight. Your Packard was front and center," somebody said.

"Yeah, remember those palm trees where we shared beer and conversation? Well, they're full of lead. If it wasn't for Emma—"

"I know. I almost pinched her at the city limits on her way down. She's getting accustomed to those armored vehicles you like, isn't she?"

"I wouldn't know about that. You'll have to ask her."

Nancy called from the kitchen. "Come on, people. It's ready. Come and get it or Luz and I will throw it out."

The doorbell rang, and Don hurried to greet the newcomer. "Come on in. The gang's all here and raring to eat."

He leaned out the door and eyed the shiny SUV in the driveway parked behind Jim's derelict Packard.

"Nice ride."

"Thanks, Don."

"You should talk to Nash about scoring one of those." He chuckled and closed the door behind Emma, smiling at his comment.

Chapter 32

Nancy looked around her kitchen, satisfied the food bomb that went off fed everyone, kept them talking and laughing, and finally, made them all retreat to the back yard. The dogs had a time of it, running from one guest to the other, fearful that they might miss out on something only they knew about.

She retreated wordlessly into the house, not wanting anyone to see her leave and think it was cleanup time. No one ever allowed her to do it alone. Even Don and Jim, pretending to grumble about being forced to do woman's work, as they called it, always helped. Besides, she knew they weren't serious, anyway. If they were, she and Maddie would have stabbed them in the back.

She snickered at the thought.

Don caught her out laughing out loud, but she shrugged it off. She retreated to the small office in the back of the house, where she went through the papers one last time. She debated repeatedly with herself. Forced herself to take a hard look. Went through the familiar papers again and again.

Only Jim knew. She confided in him when they were down in Mexico. Knew she could trust him to keep what he knew to himself. Still, confession to the man or not, it was time. It was long past time.

Nancy called to the girl. That she still thought of Luz as a girl, even after all these years, was no surprise. In her mind, Luz was a girl. Even if she was all grown up and a woman now.

Luz was busy laughing at something Emma said. She stood up and nodded in Nancy's direction before making for the kitchen.

"You are so pretty in that dress, Luz," she said.

"Thank you. I am so grateful to Tricia for helping you to fix it. I was ready to—"

"I know you were. That's why I took it upon myself to rescue it. Tricia was so excited about helping with it. Now come with me. There is something I want to show you."

Nancy wasn't certain she was doing the right thing. It was a lifetime ago when she gave the girl up for adoption. She was too young. Her boyfriend was too young. It wouldn't have worked. All those things and more, she told herself then, even up to this very day.

Luz followed her to the small office. Nancy closed the door and gestured to the chair. Luz sat down. Nancy pulled her chair from behind the desk to the side in order to remove the barrier between them.

"There are some papers I want you to look at after I tell you a story."

Nancy clutched the files to her chest and began.

Chapter 33

Luz had some difficulty understanding what Nancy was trying to tell her. She listened, though. Didn't interrupt. She trusted the woman. Nancy had taken her in without question when she first arrived. Because she got to know her when Jim brought Nancy to help get her back from Mexico. Because Nancy went beyond her duty to get her back.

She considered Nancy's background, still unsure of what that was, exactly. She suspected it was something with some three-letter government agency. She couldn't be sure, of course. She didn't think she would ever be sure. Or know.

She thought back to how Nancy went to the trouble of locating her when she wanted to have her come to Tricia's party. The girl wanted to show her the dress she had repaired for her. Nancy made it very plain that she was to attend. She didn't say *Or else*, but it was implied.

Following the request, Nancy had disappeared

into a crowd, just as she herself would have done.

Either the woman was a spy, or still was a spy, or a killer. She went with both. Spy and killer. And then wondered if Don, Nancy's husband, knew.

Nancy finished speaking and held out the folder, interrupting her thoughts. "All the information is here. Would you like to take it with you to examine?"

Luz didn't answer right away. She was having some trouble digesting what Nancy had just told her. Instead, she deflected, and brought up the invitation she received to move into Jim's building.

Nancy didn't hesitate. "He's a good man. It's obvious you both care about each other in a professional way. You saved his life on the Baja. It didn't even take him a minute to decide he needed to get you out of Mexico."

"Yet you insisted on coming with him."

Nancy agreed. "And I think you know why, now." Nancy sealed the envelope. "I'm going to put this away." She wrote *For Luz* on it before opening a desk drawer. She deposited the envelope before sliding it shut and locking it. She reached across the desk with the key.

"This is yours now. There is only one. It's not the most secure lock, but Don knows not to ask too many questions about my life."

Luz looked at Nancy, studying her. She recognized the pain in her face. "You have not told him."

"No. I have not."

"Will you tell him?" Luz asked.

"That is entirely up to you, Luz. You need to look at the papers first. Then it will be a decision for you to make."

Nancy appeared relieved, as did Luz. "There is one thing you need to know. I told Jim. He knows."

Luz nodded, satisfied. Jim's lips would be sealed. She didn't need to ask Nancy. She trusted Jim with her life. As he trusted her.

"Very well. I will consider what you have told me. If I need to see the papers for myself, I will ask."

Luz accepted the key and stood up, ready to leave. "I know it was a very difficult thing for you to do, Nancy. I will try to understand. That is all I can say for now."

Luz said her goodbyes to everyone, making sure to hug Tricia and pet Lola. Both girl and dog followed her to her bicycle. The pair were inseparable, and she thought Jim made a wise decision to give up the dog to a good home with Tricia to fuss over the dog. Not that Jim's home wasn't good, of course.

Luz grinned down at girl and dog as she said her goodbyes for a second time.

Chapter 34

It was almost too late.

Luz cursed under her breath for being lax. If she hadn't had so much occupying her thoughts following her sit-down with Nancy. If she hadn't decided to skip the bus and ride her bike home. All she wanted to do was use the time to consider what Nancy told her.

It was a quick check in her mirrors that brought the tail to her attention. That, and a seeming change-up when a rider veered off onto a side street while the other continued behind her. She made a simple adjustment to her balaclava. The movement covered everything but her eyes.

She took her time examining her surroundings. Spotted a bicycle shop's sign and turned off into the empty lot out front. It was a familiar ruse. She had successfully used it once before.

Luz kicked down the side-stand and dismounted. Immediately she bent down, pretending to tie an errant lace. Her hands found razor-sharp blades in familiar locations. She slipped them silently from their supple leather sheaths. The motion concealed them within the specially outfitted sleeves of her jacket.

She straightened and looked to the store's silver-colored window. It provided an almost mirror-perfect view of the ground and street behind her. She checked in all directions and finally caught sight of the rider. He made to ride past and then braked hard to pull into the far end of the lot. He coasted toward her before halting too close for her liking.

She couldn't do anything about that. Instead, she moved to the window and raised a hand to shade her view. It gave her a clear picture of what she needed to do.

"Those are some nice-looking rides, aren't they?" the man said.

Her riding companion set his bike on the kickstand and dismounted. He moved to her left side. She adjusted her angle and saw a dark-complexioned male. Straight oily hair. Mexican, no doubt. She thought she detected a Mexican accent. It made it so much easier. That, and the bulge beneath his left arm. It was plainly visible in the window.

She cast an errant glance at her ride, scarred and scraped and taped and unwashed. A beater, some called it. Definitely not worth stealing. It was why she kept it that way. "I wish I could afford a new one."

The man's hand moved to reach for the zipper on his jacket. In one smooth motion he reached inside. Not too fast. Not to slow. The movement revealed the butt of the handgun hanging beneath his left arm.

Luz was quicker. She pushed on his right elbow. His hand moved past the butt of the handgun. It rotated his torso partially to the left. A knife flashed in her right hand. She stepped aside, bent both knees, straightened, and slashed. The knife traveled neck-high in a wide arc and connected.

She stepped away. Avoided the gushing blood. Brought her left up and slashed a second time. She connected again. Her attacker collapsed against the window and slipped to the ground, leaving a trail of blood on the window. He raised both hands and circled his neck in a futile attempt to curb the flow of blood.

It was finished.

Luz considered his move. He was stupid. He should have approached from the right. He could have shot her without even withdrawing his weapon. She shrugged and ran her gloved hands over the body. Found what she was looking for. Pocketed it and rode off as fast as she could.

When she was clear, she halted in a mini-mall and withdrew the phone. It wasn't even locked. Sloppy. There were no recent calls or texts. She tossed it into the bed of a passing half-ton and rode off.

Her only concern was for number two. Where was he, and what would she find on his phone?

She rode for hours, her eyes fixed on her six. Scanning ahead and side to side. Desperate for a sighting, she missed a red light. Tires screeched. She avoided the car at the last minute. She stopped. Shuddered. Waited. Circled back. Stopped and waited some more. There was nothing. Nobody.

She sighed with relief and cycled the rest of the way home.

She would need to get rid of her bike. Her clothes. The knives. Everything.

She showered in a rush. Packed up the clothes she was wearing, including her boots, in a laundry bag. Made sure everything was wiped that needed to be wiped. She tied the laundry bag on the front of her bike and pedaled in the directions of the causeway. It was early. Traffic was at a minimum. She halted half-way. Heaved the bike to the railing. Pushed it over. She never heard it splash.

She tossed the clean knives with a gloved hand. They joined the bike.

She began to walk and then jog, making for the homeless part of the city. It took her half an hour. She was rewarded when she saw a drum with a fire burning. She nodded to two miserable denizens and threw the laundry bag into the fire. She waited longer than she wanted, but when she left, there was nothing remaining of her clothes and boots.

Nothing but ashes.

Chapter 35

Luz found herself with more to worry about than moving into the Nash building, as she called it. She was concerned someone might have discovered where she lived. That she was being watched. If they found her, she wouldn't be long for this world. She had to act immediately, and quickly, before the situation got away from her.

There was something else, though. She was returning from Nancy's place when she picked up on the tail. That wasn't good. Did they, whoever they were, know she was at Nancy's? Were they watching the Boyle residence, too?

It was almost overwhelming. If the Boyle home was compromised—

She changed clothes quickly. Replaced the knives. Made sure her firearms were loaded and at the ready. Two Model 71s. A single suppressed automatic. Spare magazines for each.

She donned fresh boots, making certain the

knives were in place. Satisfied, she slipped into the backpack. Checked that everything was within easy reach. It was all comfortable, for time after time she made the same checks. She never tired of doing it. How many years had it been, and always the same? Like a perfectly fitted suit of clothes. Except, she was a sicario. The tools of her trade were everything to her.

She smiled, recalling the clothes Anya presented to her after they made safe harbor south of Todos. They were too big for her, but she had adjusted some to fit. Others she kept aside for when she was older.

The smile of remembrance froze on her face. Just when she was thinking everything was slowing down. That she could begin to enjoy her new life and her friends. It was looking like it wasn't as settled as she thought. If that was the case, she would make them pay again. As many times as it took.

Lobo wasn't dead.

The beater started first try. The tank was full. The oil was fresh. She was ready. She made for the Boyle neighborhood. She parked on the edge. The car wouldn't look out of place. It was older, but the paint was fresh and it appeared well cared for. She got out, donned her backpack, and began walking.

Her trained eye took in everything. Scanned for anything out of the ordinary. She stopped to take a drink. Halted and pretended to adjust boot laces. Removed her backpack and pretended to search.

Came up with an energy bar. Walked some more. Halted to replace the water and the bar before continuing on.

So far, so good.

Until she spotted the black Navigator.

Tinted windows made it impossible to tell how many were inside. In an instant, she decided. Immediately, she turned and began jogging back to her car. It was a chance she had to take. The SUV could be gone by the time she returned. It could be replaced by another. Different make. Different model.

If she was lucky, if-if-if too many ifs.

She almost yelled with joy when she climbed into her car. She slammed the door with a satisfying thunk and headed for the street where she discovered the SUV.

Hoping turned to wishing turned to needing, and then there it was. Almost as though it was still there on purpose.

Did they know about her?

<h1 style="text-align:center">Chapter 36</h1>

Luz **didn't pick up** on her shadow right away. Whoever it was, they were that good. Or she was getting that sloppy. It took her way too long to realize she even had a tail. When she did, it was the walk.

The walk gave it all away.

Nancy. It was Nancy. On the opposite side of the street.

Did Nancy spot her in the car? She would have to ask later. For now, there was no sign of recognition. Nothing passed between them. There was no need. Two professionals. Doing their jobs. Whatever was required.

Whatever it was.

Luz opened the door quietly and donned her backpack for a second time. Instinctively, she checked her weapons reach. Satisfied, she allowed the door to swing silently on oiled hinges. Didn't latch it closed. Immediately, she took off, following Nancy. How long was it? It couldn't be more than a couple of minutes. She knew without even thinking about it.

Nancy had made her. Whatever the woman was, she was that good. Maybe even better than her. If that was the case, what had Nancy been capable of in her former job?

The woman stepped off the sidewalk and disappeared right in front of her. She jogged toward the spot. She had to be lying in wait. She listened. Heard tongue-clicking. Turned. There she was. Face to face with a woman she did not want to trifle with, under any circumstance.

There was no sign of recognition. No hello. There was only a question.

"Did you see them?"

Nancy would know she did.

"Yes. Two. Professionals."

No chit-chat.

"Agreed. You or me?"

Luz didn't hesitate. "I will do it. You will back me up."

There was no hesitation when Nancy replied. "Yes."

Chapter 37

Luz unzipped her jacket, exposing the twin Model 71s. One was in a shoulder holster beneath her left arm. The other was in a holster clipped to her belt, on her front right side. The grip faced left. If she had to, she could fill both hands.

"Undo the top of my backpack, por favor." She turned away from Nancy. The woman did as Luz asked. She reached up and over her shoulder. Her hand closed on the familiar handgun's grip. Satisfied, she withdrew her hand. The Model 17 disappeared from sight.

"Thank you. We will go now."

She smiled at Nancy. It was a smile quickly returned by a look of determination from the woman.

Luz headed off at a trot toward the SUV. After a block, she did a shoulder check. Nancy was at her seven. She nodded and smiled inwardly, satisfied. She knew not to expect anything less from the woman.

They reached the street. The SUV was still on

station. Immediately, they separated. Nancy crossed to the sidewalk on the opposite side. Luz saw the woman withdraw her handgun. She slowed to a walk. Between parked cars, she witnessed Nancy screwing on the suppressor.

Luz continued on course, street-side, to the parked cars. She reached into a pocket on the side of her backpack and withdrew a small black hammer. She looped it onto her right wrist. Her left hand went to her waist and closed on the .22 caliber Long Rifle automatic.

Twenty feet.

Ten.

She shoulder-checked for Nancy. Didn't see her. That was good.

The front windows were much stronger than those on the rear doors on these new vehicles. She had learned that years ago, the hard way. It almost cost her life.

Luz pulled up her right arm to cross her body. She swung the hammer in a wide arc. It connected with the SUV's window. The glass shattered instantly. It gave her the element of surprise.

She looked in. Pulled the gun's trigger twice on the passenger. Swiveled to the right until her hip bumped the SUV and pulled it twice again.

There was silence but for the idling engine.

She opened the driver's door. Without hesitating, she gave him two more before doing the same to the passenger. No interior light switched on. The street light illuminated the passenger's dead hands. His hands gripped a suppressed Mac-10 lying across his lap.

She went through the pockets of the driver as best she could. There was no phone. On the opposite side, Nancy did the same with the passenger and shook her head.

Luz unlocked all the doors and Nancy got into the back. Together they pulled and wrestled and pushed and finally wrestled the driver into the back. They did the same with the passenger.

They paused and caught their breath after climbing into the front seats.

Nancy drove.

"All right. Let's go."

"I need to get rid of my weapon," Luz told her.

"I know. Coming right up," Nancy said.

Luz dropped the magazine and cleared the handgun before wiping it down. She made sure to tuck the magazine into her backpack.

"There's a city garbage truck up ahead. We'll toss it there."

It wasn't what Luz wanted for the firearm.

Nancy recognized her concern. "Don't worry. In a week it will be buried so deep no one will find it."

Luz wasn't convinced. She said nothing.

"We need a container for gasoline and a shady gas station if we're going to get rid of this thing. Start wiping while I start looking."

Nancy eased past the refuse truck and slowed to a halt beside a bin in the truck's path. "Toss it here and we're good to go."

Luz quickly stripped the pistol and did as she was told. Still, she wasn't happy. She would rather have tossed her pistol into the ocean.

"I know what you're thinking, but you'll see. The

gun will be gone, and so will we."

Nancy steered for the south end of the city. "We'll find what we're looking for here."

She came up on an unfenced junk yard and got out. When she returned, she carried two plastic containers. She opened the tailgate and dropped the sloshing jugs. "

"There was an overhead tank in the back. I need a screwdriver."

Luz bent to reach into her boot to retrieve a knife. She handed it off to Nancy. Immediately the woman pried the registration plate from the dashboard and handed the knife back. "That should do it."

It took the pair ten minutes of driving to find the perfect area. There were no lights. No cameras they could see. No gates to pass through. Nancy halted the vehicle and got out.

Luz opened a jug of gasoline in the front seat while Nancy did the same in the back. There was no time to admire their handiwork. A lit match ended up tossed into the back and the SUV was engulfed in flames almost instantly.

The pair trotted off at a pace fast enough to get them far enough away to ensure questions wouldn't be asked. Eventually, sirens blared behind them. Blue and red lights flashed.

"Follow me." Nancy led Luz into a dark alley, where the pair got out of their coveralls and balaclavas. Gloves followed. They waited without talking while another match and a brief wait made sure there was nothing left but ashes.

"We can walk normally now. I know the city. We will be home before you know it." Nancy pulled a wig out of her backpack and moved to hand it to Luz. "Put this on. We'll be taking public transit all the way."

"No need. I have my own," Luz said.

Chapter 38

Nancy and Luz double-timed it in search of a bus stop. They agreed on one and settled on the bench to wait it out.

"There is something I need to ask you, Nancy."

Nancy held her breath as a million things ran through her mind, but she settled on only one. It was the discussion she had with Luz earlier in the day.

"Jim and Maddie have asked if I would like to move into their building."

Nancy exhaled. "They have? Do they have room?"

Nancy pictured the building and its three floors. As far as she knew, there was not a lot of room on level two or three for another residence. The bottom was vacant. She didn't know why Jim didn't rent it.

"Yes. Anya has completed her schooling and is moving to go to her first job. I think she is already gone."

Nancy considered before responding. Luz would

be safe with Jim and Maddie. Emma was in the building. That was a plus, too. She even thought about Friday and how Luz got along with Maddie's dog. "How do you feel about it? Do you think the building will be safe?"

"I would want some changes for sure." Luz went on to list them. "Steel doors on all the upstairs apartments. Another on the fire escape exit. Intruder alarms for sure." She valued Nancy's opinion. "What do you think?"

Nancy didn't hesitate. She wanted her daughter to be safe, even if the girl wouldn't accept her concern. "I think you'll be making a wise choice if you take them up on their offer. Jim and Maddie have always been there for my family. Emma, too, as far as that goes. You'll be surrounded by good people. There is one thing, though."

She hesitated.

"I want to go through their place with you when they aren't there. Two experienced people will pick up on a lot."

"Very well. I will see to it after I talk with Jim. He is still—"

Nancy held up a hand. "No need to explain. Call when you're ready and we'll go through the details together. There is one thing, though."

"Si?"

"Don't mention it to Jim."

"No problemo."

A loud whistle pierced the night. Nancy went on alert. She reached for her automatic and the suppressor and began screwing it on. "This is not good, Luz. That sounds like a signal."

The whistle sounded again. Luz got up and stepped to the curb. She extended her arm. Her palm went flat and she extended it in the direction of the sound.

"It is all right."

Chapter 39

Nancy **was on full** alert. She held the suppressed automatic down at her side. Waiting. Her head twisted to scan in all directions to pick up what she perceived as danger. The SUV advanced toward them at a crawl. She looked at Luz. She was relaxed and smiling. She took a cue from that. Still, she kept the automatic at the ready, down by her side.

"What's going on, Luz?"

The black SUV pulled to the curb beside them. A dark window rolled down without making a sound. A smiling Jim Nash greeted them. Nancy looked across the seat to witness Emma behind the wheel. An even bigger smile was pasted across the young woman's face.

"What are you two doing out here—"

"No worries, ladies," Jim interrupted. "Jump in."

Nancy and Luz climbed into the back. Jim twisted in the front seat to face them. "Wow. These fancy leather seats make that easy. Good choice on the interior, girl. Emma here was out for a test drive in the company SUV. She invited me to come along for moral support."

Jim kept the suppressed HK MP5 out of sight. He released the rack and cleared the firearm.

Nancy recognized the sound. She had some experience with the weapon.

"We made a corporate decision and decided the only help you needed was a bus ride home. Not to mention that Emma is now happy to know she isn't the only woman in these parts to set fire to a car and have a witness to it. Is there anything you two need?"

"Dammit, Nash. You scared the crap out of me until Luz started smiling. Even then, I wasn't so sure."

Nancy cleared her own weapon and began unscrewing the suppressor. She finished and tucked both into her backpack. She completed the task as flashing blues turned on behind them.

"No problemo. Emma has all the temporary paper she needs for this tank. Right? And if she doesn't, I do for sure."

Emma slowed and pulled the huge vehicle into a well-lit parking lot where a barista advertised 24-hour fancy coffees.

"You all know the drill, peeps," Jim said. "Hands on seat backs and dashboard."

Emma's sweaty hands gripped the top of the steering wheel while she waited for the officer to approach. He kept his distance, approaching from the left rear.

"Good evening. What are you all up to tonight?"

Emma twisted her head in the voice's direction

and flashed white teeth in a friendly smile. "Well, officer, it's this way. We had a hankerin' for some fine coffee, and this place came up in the conversation. It came up on the GPS, too. I thought I'd try it with my friends."

"Hankerin'? I haven't heard that word used in forever. Where are you from, ma'am?"

Emma's grin grew even wider. "I'm hardly a ma'am, officer. And I'm from Colorado. It's a fine word we use out there when we have to have something and we don't want to wait."

Luz squirmed in her seat and put her hands in her lap.

"Sit still, *hija*. Put your hands back on the seat, por favor," Nancy instructed.

Jim's jaw dropped. Nancy just called Luz daughter. He was about to say something to make light of the word when the officer waved them on their way.

"Have a nice evening. Enjoy your coffee. It's not a bad place if they have what you want at this early hour."

Emma stuck her head out the window. "Where are you from, officer?"

A radio call grabbed the officer's attention. His reply was lost in the static.

"Well, folks. That was interesting. What are we all getting?"

The breathing started again.

"I think we should get our collective asses home. Don will come off shift shortly and I don't want to explain why I'm out joyriding with a bunch of teenagers in a brand-new car," Nancy said.

"The woman has a point. Let's go, Emma," Jim said.

"Not before we get the coffee I promised the nice police officer we were having."

Fueled by the fresh coffee, Emma manhandled the SUV over the curb and bumped out into the street. "Sorry, guys. I'm not used to the size of this modern tank yet."

She hit the gas and rubber squealed as she pointed the car toward Nancy's neighborhood. When Emma got them to the street where the suspect SUV was parked, the vacant spot was taken by a compact car.

"Looks like we're home free. For now."

Emma turned on to the Boyle's street. Don's vehicle was already in the driveway.

"Crap. Well, you're all invited in. Be sure to bring your coffee. That was a good idea, Emma. You're on the payroll now, that's for sure."

Nancy looked at Jim. "Right, Detective Nash?"

Chapter 40

Don Boyle rattled pots and pans in the kitchen, grumbling the entire time. He chopped mushrooms and sliced tomatoes and broke eggs and added a bit of cream into the giant bowl.

Emma called out from the living room. "You need any help with that, Don?"

There was more grumbling and a gruff voice replied. "I think I can manage a few eggs and bacon. Too bad Friday isn't here to help with that. What were you teenagers up to, anyway?"

Lola, the Boyle's dog, recognized the word, *bacon*. Immediately, she deserted the crowd in the living room and trotted into the kitchen.

"Good girl, Lola. My fave dog is on my side, at least." He reached to give her a pet and resumed fussing over the stove after wiping his hand.

"If that Nash character was any kind of fisherman, he'd offer to cook up some of his famous grilled cheese sammiches for all of us. Right, Lola?"

A sleepy Tricia poked her head around the corner. "Dad. What are you doing? It's too early for breakfast."

"Did you happen to look in the living room, daughter? The gang's all here and they're hungry. They didn't even bring me a coffee for my troubles."

Nancy used the fuss to make for the basement where she stowed her backpack. In minutes, she returned to the fold. "Luz, we'll look tomorrow, okay?"

Luz nodded. She was busy looking at Nancy. The *hija* comment had set her mind wandering back to her mother and father in better times. Although, these times were pretty good, too.

Tricia peeked into the living room. "Hello everybody. Where's Maddie? Where's Friday?"

Jim jumped up to take the test. "I had a report to write. Maddie is looking it over. I think she's going to get a grade of A+ if I know anything about her writing skills. And faithful dog Friday is helping her out with spelling and grammar, as always."

"Uncle Jim, dogs can't read or write. Everybody knows that."

Jim smiled down at the girl. "Don't be too sure of that, young lady. Friday is pretty smart for a dog. Why don't you give Maddie a call and see how they're doing?"

Tricia retreated to the kitchen, where she borrowed her father's phone before returning to the living room with her results. "There's no answer, Uncle Jim. I tried a bunch of times."

"That's strange. She should be there. Did you try the office phone too? Here, I'll dial it for you."

Jim dialed and waited for the phone to ring. He handed it back to Tricia.

Tricia listened, and held up the phone. "There's no answer there, either, Uncle Jim."

Jim endured breakfast only long enough until he could gather Luz and Emma in the living room. "We need to go. Now. Maddie isn't picking up."

He made a quick stop in the Boyle kitchen to say goodbye.

Don looked up at his friend. "Let us know what you find out, Nash. Maddie and Friday are part of our family, too, even if you won't admit it."

"Oh yes. We know that. Considering recent developments— nothing serious. Just— just—"

Jim looked at Nancy.

"She's not there."

**Want to find out what happened to Maddie?
Read the short story Gone to find out.**

PX DUKE

GONE

ONE

Don Boyle rattled pots and pans in the kitchen. He grumbled the entire time as he chopped mushrooms, tomato, and bacon. He broke eggs. Poured in a bit of cream. Whisked merrily away at the giant omelet.

Emma called from the living room.

"You need any help back there, Don?"

There was more grumbling and a gruff voice replied. "I think I can manage a few eggs and bacon. Too bad Friday isn't here to help with that. What were you teenagers up to, anyway?"

Lola, the Boyle's dog, recognized *bacon*. Immediately, she trotted into the kitchen and sat patiently at her master's feet.

"Good girl, Lola. My fave dog is on my side, at least." Don reached to give the dog a pat and resumed fussing over the stove as he called to the group assembled in his living room.

"If that Jim Nash character was any kind of fisherman, he'd offer to cook up some of his famous grilled cheese sammiches for all of us. Right, Lola?"

Awakened by the commotion, a sleepy Tricia made her way downstairs to investigate. She poked her head around the corner. "D-a-a-D. Did I hear sammiches? What are you doing? It's too early for breakfast."

Don grinned at his daughter, happy she was up to witness his kitchen fussing. "Did you look in the living room, daughter? The gang's all here and they're hungry. They didn't even bring me a coffee for my troubles."

Nancy used the fuss to make for the basement where she stored her backpack. In minutes, she returned to the living room to address Luz. "We'll take a look tomorrow, okay?"

Luz nodded. She was relieved Nancy would help her check out the Nash building. Before she moved in, she wanted to improve the security of the place.

She studied Nancy. The *hija* comment set her mind wandering back to better times, to her mother and father. Although, these times were good, too, since she had moved here from Mexico.

Tricia peeked into the living room. Her eyes took in the crowd and went wide. "Hello everybody." She looked around the living room. "Where's Maddie? Where's Friday?"

Jim jumped up to take the test. "So only part of the clan isn't good enough for you, young lady? I'll be talking to your dad about that, I'll have you know."

He went on before Tricia could scold him. "I had a report that needed fine tuning. Maddie is looking it over. I think she's going to get an A+ grade if I know anything about her writing skills. And faithful dog Friday is helping her out, as always."

"Uncle Jim, dogs can't read or write. Everybody knows that."

Jim smiled down at the girl. "Don't be too sure about that, young lady. Friday is pretty smart for a dog. Why don't you give Maddie a call and see how they're doing? I'm pretty sure she'd like an invitation to the party."

Tricia retreated to the kitchen, where she borrowed her father's phone before returning to the living room with her results. "There's no answer, Uncle Jim. I tried a bunch of times."

"That's strange. She should be there. Did you try the office phone too? Here, I'll dial it for you." Jim waited for it to ring before handing the phone back to Tricia.

She took it and listened and finally held the phone up. "There's no answer there, either, Uncle Jim."

Don called the crowd to order with his announcement. "Come and get it or you're never invited back."

Hungry friends gorged on Don's omelets and toast and bacon and fried tomatoes until chairs pushed back and dishes rattled in the sink.

Jim endured Don's breakfast fixings only long enough until he could gather Luz and Emma together in the living room. "I think we need to go. Maddie isn't picking up," he said.

He made a quick stop in the Boyle kitchen to say goodbye.

Don looked up at his friend. "Eat it and beat it, huh, Nash? Let us know what you find out. Maddie and Friday are part of our family, too, even if you won't bring them." He laughed.

"Yeah, we know. Considering recent developments, it's nothing serious. Just— just—"

He looked at Nancy. "She's not there."

Jim, Emma and Luz piled into Emma's new SUV.

"I'm worried," Jim said. "Take us to the office."

Emma started the car and backed into the street. "She's fine, Jim. She probably turned the phones off knowing you'd be calling to check up on her."

It was true. He had been bugging Maddie about checking his work on the report he needed to file. He had concerns about the final 50K payment due from the feds. If there was one thing he was certain of, it was that he wasn't about to get cheated out of honest pay for an honest job.

Emma wasn't driving fast enough for his liking. To take his mind off of that, he tried calling the office again. When there was no answer, he called Maddie's phone. He texted, too, but there was no response. "She's still not picking up."

Emma pulled into the empty parking spot in front of the business where his Packard usually sat. It was out for repair.

Jim left Emma and Luz in the dust and made for the building's door. He rushed up the stairs two at a time, halting at the office. The door was closed but unlocked. He rushed in to check the desks, searching for the report. It wasn't there.

He deserted the office and ran upstairs. He used his key to get past the locked door and rushed into the apartment. The report lay open on the kitchen table. It appeared Maddie had made notes on about two-thirds of it before she was called away. Friday was gone, too.

He searched the apartment looking for a note. Friday's bowls were where they should be, which meant Maddie hadn't taken the dog on an unannounced road trip.

He met the women coming up the stairs and shooed them down to the second-floor office.

"There's nothing up there. She made it through about half the report. Friday is gone, too."

Jim punched in the combination to the huge office safe and swung the heavy door wide. He hauled out the money bag and looked inside.

"It looks like there's about 20 thousand missing. Do either of you know anything about this? Did she say anything about taking on a new case? She does that sometimes when she can't get hold of me. I'm usually the last to know."

"Not a word, Jim." Emma looked at Luz. "What about you?"

"She said nothing to me."

Jim went on. "I suppose she could have taken a call and went out to meet up with someone about a case. Like I said, it's happened before. I don't see any notes though."

He shuffled random papers on Maddie's desk.

"Wait. Here's something."

TWO

Maddie Spence hung up the phone and looked down at Friday snoozing in his office bed. From there, her eyes moved back to the report on the desk in front of her. She was supposed to be finishing up with some editing. She rubbed at her eyes and blinked. "Well, Friday, it sounds like we have a road trip coming up. Are you ready?"

Already she was making a mental list. Dog food and dishes? Not needed. There would be plenty on-site. She'd throw a few toys together in a bag for her dog. Phone? Check. She pulled out a new burn phone from the desk and a charge cord. Suitcase? Check. In the upstairs closet. All she had to do was throw a few things into it.

Friday sighed in his doggie dream and rolled onto his side. His feet moved as though he were walking somewhere.

"I swear, Friday, you are far too relaxed."

She pushed back the office chair. The wheels squeaked, disturbing faithful Friday.

She picked up the report and made for upstairs and her closet and the suitcase.

Friday jumped up and seemed to give her a dirty look, as though annoyed at being disturbed.

"That's it, watchdog. Come along." She dropped the report she was supposed to be editing on the kitchen table.

Friday trotted up the stairs after his mistress. His ears perked up when he overheard her rummaging in the bedroom. He jumped up on the bed and sat down to keep an eye on things.

Maddie put the bag on the bed beside Friday and began filling it with clothes. She snapped it shut and hefted it onto the floor, where she pulled out the handle to roll it into the kitchen.

"All right. Let's see. Laptop. Phone. Doggie bag. My bag. Long and short leashes. I think we're good to go."

She filled Friday's portable water bottle with cold water. She grabbed dog treats, cold drinks and yogurt from the fridge, and walked out of the apartment. She made sure to lock the door behind her before descending to the office. She opened the gun safe, took out her Model 17 and two magazines, and locked it.

Nash's report would have to wait.

"Come on, boy. Car ride."

That was all Friday needed to hear. He trotted out the open ground-floor door to an empty parking spot. He woofed and looked up at his mistress.

"Yeah, Jim's car is gone. We're taking mine. Come along."

She extended the handle and pulled the suitcase behind her.

Friday dutifully trotted along at her side until they arrived at her compact car. Friday barked to call shotgun, and she laughed as she opened the passenger door for him. His furiously wagging tail nearly got caught when she slammed it shut.

She sent off a text announcing her arrival time, started the car, and they were on their way.

The pair stopped for water and Frisbee breaks. Still, they made Panama Crossing in jig time. Maddie pulled into the marina's parking lot. A scramble of people and dogs hurried to greet her.

She opened her door and Friday scrambled across her thighs to join the approaching noisy melee.

She quickly counted heads and sighed with relief.

Lily was there, safe and sound.

"Am I glad to see you, young lady."

An embarrassed Erica was forced to explain that Lily's cell phone died. That she hadn't called to check in. That panic had set in when no one knew where she was. That the girl had been at a friend's place having too much fun riding horses.

"I panicked when I couldn't get in touch with her," Erica said. "My first thought was to call you and Jim, Maddie. I'm so sorry to bring you all this way on a false alarm. I tried calling you to let you know—"

Maddie held up a hand and smiled at Erica. "First of all, there's no need to apologize. I'm just happy to learn Lily is fine." She looked across the parking lot at Friday. "Judging by my dog's reaction, he's happy to see everyone."

Friday busied himself running circles around dogs and people he hadn't seen for ages. Sniffing and snuffling and giggles and laughs followed his antics as he attempted to renew acquaintances all at once.

"I'm sorry I scared you, Auntie Maddie," Lily said. "My phone— my phone—"

"We all make mistakes, Lily. And we all learn the hard way about those darned phone batteries, too. I'm glad to see you, even so. It's been a while."

She hugged the girl.

Jealous Friday crawled through legs and sniffed and snuffled at the pair as he nosed and licked hands and fingers.

Lily giggled at the dog's antics and his cold nose.

James sidled up to Maddie.

Friday had no mercy for the boy, either. He laughed and got down on one knee and hugged the dog.

"Will you tell Uncle Jim that we're taking care of Zelda for him, Maddie?"

Maddie looked down at the boy. "Funny you should mention that. I was just thinking of taking a walk to sit beneath the tree for a bit before I head for home. Why don't you come along?"

Maddie made her way up the slight rise to the house trailer and the shade tree with the kids and the dogs.

"Be careful, Auntie Maddie," James warned. "You don't want to step on Zelda's tail."

Friday chose that moment to woof and nudge her thigh with his cold nose. She jumped and laughed nervously.

"I'll be careful."

"Zelda would woof just like Friday did when that happened," James said. "Zelda didn't get angry, though. She would lick our hands and we'd tell her we were sorry, and she always forgave us."

Maddie checked the time. "Why don't you two keep Friday company while I go down and see Allie and Warren? I won't be long."

Maddie headed off to say her goodbyes and walked back up the hill.

Friday was happily ensconced between Lily and James. He was on his back getting belly rubs and scratches.

"You're spoiling my dog, you two. Now give me a hug so I can get going. It's going to be a long drive in the night by the time I get home."

Allie and Erica and the kids followed her to the car. "Thank you so much for coming, Maddie. I know it must have been a pain to drive all that way, only to learn Lily was fine."

"Not at all. You've helped Jim and me countless times by providing a safe house for the Boyle's daughter, Tricia. It would have helped if I had turned on my phone. I was so worried and eager to get here—"

"That's what friends are for. Now drive carefully. Would you like us to call Jim and let him know you're on your way home?"

"Yes, please. I'm supposed to be working on a report so we can get paid for a job. He's probably wondering where I got to. Come to think of it, he has no idea where I am."

THREE

Jim Nash checked the display on his ringing phone. "Hello, Erica. How are you? It's been a while." They went back and forth until Erica finally revealed why she was calling.

"So that's where she got to. I've been worrying about that woman. She hasn't bothered to pick up. It's probably not even turned on."

Erica went on. "She rushed out here in a hurry, and we're grateful for that. She's headed home now. She didn't even take time for a snack. I managed to brown-bag some sandwiches for her and Friday. Lily gave them some of Zelda's doggie cookies, too."

"Talk about a flying trip," he said. "I'm glad Lily is all right. We owe you all for what you do for us, so never hesitate to call if something isn't right. That's what we're here for. I'll text when she gets home."

Jim didn't text when Maddie got home. He

waited. Checked the time too many times. Called her number. Of course it went to voicemail. He was so annoyed by sun-up he went down the hall to bang on Emma's door.

A faint voice filtered past it. "It's early for breakfast, Nash. This better be good." She opened the door and let him in.

"I'm taking the SUV and heading out to the marina. I haven't been able to get in touch with Maddie—"

Emma held up a hand. "Wait. What? She's been out there? Whatever for?"

Jim explained what happened with Lily. "It's all good. Lily is home safe. Now it's Maddie that's missing."

Emma followed Jim to the office, where he opened the safe. Maddie's firearm was gone. That made sense. She would have taken it with her.

He dragged out the bag of cash and looked inside again. It looked like about 20K was missing, but he couldn't be certain. He handed 10 thousand to Emma.

"Call it traveling money. I have to travel. You have to stay here and man the barricades when you're not at your regular job."

Emma nodded.

"Oh, and I'm going to need your SUV, too," he added.

"Not a problem. I still have the Jeep for a bit," she told him.

Jim dialed Luz's number.

She picked up right away.

"I need your services if you're available," he said.

He didn't tell her Maddie was missing. He didn't think it was right to put that kind of pressure on her. That, and they had just invited her to move into their building.

"I'm ready," Luz said. "I'll meet where we usually do. Will the Model 17 and my Model 71s be sufficient?"

"Yes. See you soon."

Jim was at the meet-up twenty minutes later. Luz was waiting.

"Thanks for agreeing, Luz. Maddie has gone missing." He explained what happened with Lily. That Maddie was headed back from the marina. She hadn't showed and was past due. That she wasn't picking up her phone. That it wasn't unusual."

"She took 20 thousand in cash. Traveling money, we call it. Just in case. She wasn't taking any chances with Lily missing."

"But the girl is all right now, yes?" Luz asked.

"Yes, she's safe. Apparently, Lily and a friend rode their bikes to go horseback riding. They were all excited and forgot the time and with the grooming and everything, her phone went dead and, well, you know how it goes with kids."

He regretted saying it immediately. Luz didn't know how it went with children. Her childhood had been brutally taken from her.

"What of Maddie? Do you know where she is?" Luz asked.

Of course he didn't know where Maddie was. That's not what he said. "She left the marina to head home. She had sandwiches and food and water for Friday."

"I think she would be in a hurry to get home. Perhaps she would only stop for bathroom breaks."

That was true. He would do the same.

"Coffee. That would be one break, too. You have driven that route, have you not? Where might she stop?" Luz asked.

There was only one place. And it was very familiar to both him and Maddie. But she might stop for a sleep, too. Maddie was accustomed to sleeping in her car, even though she hadn't been doing anything like it for so many years, he couldn't remember. She might think of it as a bit of an adventure with Friday.

"You might as well grab some shuteye, Luz. We're going to be a while."

She climbed over the seat and stretched out in the back. "I am ready if I am needed."

Jim had no doubt of that.

FOUR

Maddie already knew where her next stop was going to be. Blue Springs. She knew the street. Knew the coffee shop. Even knew the town had a familiar motel if she wanted to sleep in comfort.

She wouldn't be stopping for anything beyond a coffee for herself and fresh water for Friday, though. Friday would get a treat, too, although not a big one. She didn't like to see him with anything sweeter than the little bits of toast and jam Jim sneaked down to him beneath their breakfast table.

"We've got a break coming up, Friday. I'll get a coffee and you'll get a treat. How would you like that?"

Friday recognized the sound of the word treat and sat up in the back seat where he had been snoozing. It was almost like he had an ear tuned to the word, even in sleep. He woofed his approval.

Maddie turned off at the exit and made for the center of town. The hurricane and the damage it did when it swept through had been cleared away. The place actually looked normal and livable. Considering what happened to them on their visit to rescue Emma, she was surprised she could admit it.

She halted across the street from the coffee shop, beside a small park. She opened the door to let Friday out. He stretched and jumped down and stretched again before rolling in the grass.

"I know, Friday. It's tough being cooped up in a car for so long. I feel the same way." She stretched too, before finding the Frisbee in the back seat. "Time for a piddle and some exercise, favorite dog of mine."

She smiled, remembering Jim's excitement when the small puppy Friday found peed on the newspaper spread on the kitchen floor. She had teased him about it, and here she was, using the same expression.

Friday trotted to a nearby tree and raised a leg to do his own piddling. He finished and trotted back to his mistress.

"Good boy."

He sat at her feet and looked up, expectantly. He wanted that Frisbee any way he could get it. He raised one foot, and then the other, stamping them to force his mistress to throw the toy.

Finally, she tossed it. It arced and dropped to the ground. Friday jumped and pawed the grass, all while looking up at his mistress.

"Fetch," she commanded.

The dog barked and raced off in hot pursuit. He located the Frisbee. Not content with that, he wrestled with it. Grabbed it. Tossed it away and grabbed for it again before trotting back to his mistress with head held high. As he drew closer, his tail began wagging furiously.

"Here's my proud boy. What did you bring me?"

The frisky dog refused to hand over the toy right away. He lunged back and forth. Shook his head out of the way each time his mistress reached for it. It was a familiar game for both.

"Oh, look. It's a Frisbee. I swear, Friday, if you could, you'd toss that Frisbee and wait for me to retrieve it."

They went back and forth until he finally gave up the toy. Satisfied, he sat and waited for her to throw it again.

She pretended to fake him, but he was too smart for that.

He waited.

Barked.

Finally, the toy was in the air and he chased after it, again and again as they played the game.

"All right, dog. How about we take a break and let you have some water?"

He was ready. He carried the Frisbee to the car and waited.

Maddie got out the dog water bottle and let him have his fill. He snorted and lapped and licked and finished the bottle.

"You were thirsty. I bet you're hungry, too. Neither of us has had anything since the marina. I think Allie made some sandwiches for us. And Lily made some doggie cookies just for you."

She made him sit behind the car. It was out of

sight of the coffee shop. "Friday. Stay," she ordered. "I'll be right back."

He followed her to the back of the car.

"Friday. Sit. Stay."

Maddie headed off across the street. She looked back from the other side. Her faithful dog's eyes were on her all the way to the door, where she disappeared.

His mistress was out of sight, but she wasn't out of mind. Friday wasn't happy. He barked. Still, he obeyed.

And waited.

FIVE

Billy Denver's head almost twisted around like an owl when he recognized the woman's reflection in the coffee shop mirror. He had to look twice to be certain. That's how long it had been.

He realized his mistake when the woman glanced his way and then turned back. His shoulders hunched over his coffee, but his eyes remained glued to the woman's reflection in the huge mirror behind the counter.

The woman's image had been burned into his memory when the episode with his girlfriend ended with her in a wheelchair. Fiona Lubinski had ended up back in prison, too, but that was a matter for another time.

He was certain the woman hadn't recognized him. What was she doing here? How did she get here? Was there something he didn't know? What was going on? What was it all about? He was pretty confident it had to be something with Fiona. How could it not? She was housed at the woman's prison, after all. And he visited her there ever since the misunderstanding, as he liked to call it.

Fiona had to be getting a parole hearing. That had to be it. Funny she never mentioned it the last time he visited. Well, he was going to have a surprise announcement on his next visit, that was for sure.

Billy felt for the leather case and the razor-sharp knife he always carried on his belt. He tugged at the snap. The leather flap hung loose. The knife was free. He would be able to pull it out in an instant. The tang he attached to the blade made sure it would open instantly with a simple flip of his thumb and wrist. He ought to know. He spent hours practicing the motion and even more hours working the action until it was butter-smooth.

Billy swung back and forth on the stool. His eyes never left the reflection in the mirror. His feet bounced on the rail. Perspiration ran down his back, soaking his shirt. He checked his own reflection in the mirror and almost didn't recognize the man staring back.

He knew then what he would do.

Maddie saw the man staring at her reflection in the mirror. For an instant, he seemed vaguely familiar. She forgot about him as she got in line for her coffee and a treat she could share with Friday.

She settled on ordering a mocha and a biscotti for Friday. It was the closest thing resembling a nice crunchy dog biscuit, so she went with it, even though it was too sweet for him.

Something pointed and sharp dug into her side. A man's breath exhaled into her ear.

"Come with me. Now."

Maddie recognized a knife blade when its reflection flashed in the mirror. The man holding it against her was the same one she had noticed and ignored when she walked in. Whatever this was, she was in for it now.

She left her unpaid order on the counter, hoping the cashier would notice she didn't pick it up. If this man, whoever he was, planned on taking her out the front door, Friday would make short work of him.

That didn't happen. He shoved her in the direction of the back door. So much for plan A.

The cashier called out. "You leaving already, Billy? You usually stay longer."

Billy, whoever he was, ignored the woman.

He gripped her arm harder and shoved her toward the back door. He forced it open. It slammed against the brick wall and rebounded. It caught her in the shoulder and forced her against the knife.

She tried to step aside and put some distance between the knife and her side. It didn't work. He was too fast. He anticipated the move.

She felt the knife dig in and knew without looking. She was bleeding.

It was bad news to get into a stranger's vehicle. Victims usually ended up raped or worse. She couldn't do a thing with the knife still pressing against her side.

He handed her the keys. "Get in the truck and drive. I'll tell you where to go."

She drove. The town wasn't so big that she lost

track of the coffee shop she was forced to leave behind. When she turned into a long gravel driveway leading to an old house, she knew exactly where to run if she could only get away.

So far, she kept her mouth shut and obeyed orders. Was now the time to ask? She went for it. "What is it you want?" Her sweaty hands were clamped onto the steering wheel.

"You'll find out when it's time, missy."

Missy. The guy was a hillbilly. Billy the hillbilly. She went for the direct approach. "Where you from?"

"That's none of your business."

She regretted not picking up the burn phone to let Jim know where she stopped.

She tried again. "Don't you think your captor should know why she's being held against her will? Kidnapped, that is?"

He ignored her. "Turn right."

How could she have been so silly? But then, she didn't expect to get snatched off the street. Or the coffee shop. Wasn't that the place Emma worked at when she was here? She couldn't remember.

"Take the road to the end. Stop at the house."

Tires crunched on the gravel driveway. She hit the brakes too hard and skidded to a stop.

Billy reached across her to open the door. He pushed her out of the truck and slid after her on the bench seat. Blood from the wound dripped onto the gravel. The knife wound was deeper than she thought.

"Walk up to the house and go inside," Billy ordered.

The knife remained pressed to her side. Whoever he was, he knew what he was doing. She wondered how many times he had done the same thing.

Maddie hesitated inside the door. He shoved her down the hall into the kitchen. He raised a trap door and gestured with the knife.

She went down the steps, as slow as she could. The light flipped on and, for the first time, she saw what she would be in for.

SIX

Friday sensed there was something wrong. His mistress never returned with the treat she promised. He trotted off to raise his leg a final time. Trotted back to the car. Stuck his face past the car. There were no cars that would run him over.

His ears faced forward. His tail stretched out straight behind him. He was ready.

He crossed the street and made for the open door. It was the door where he last saw his mistress. He slowed momentarily before scampering in. Raised his head to test the air. His nose went to the floor. He followed a familiar scent to a door in the back of the room. It was closed.

He barked. No one came to open it.

He retraced his steps to the front door and trotted around the side of the building, all the way to the back. The scent ended. He stopped. Confused, he circled around to the front and trotted through the open door a second time before making his way to the back of the room and the closed door.

Once again he exited and circled around to the back. The familiar scent was gone.

Friday scampered across the street to the car. Still there was no mistress. He straightened his tail and laid his ears forward. He raised his head. His nose tested the air.

He listened before crossing the street. He circled the block. He went down the alley. He trotted up driveways, sniffing and snorting the entire time. When he finished with one block, he moved on to the next, where he did the same to each of the driveways leading up to the houses.

It was exhausting work, made all the more difficult by the length of time it took and the energy expended, to find his mistress. He hadn't eaten. He had no water. His paws were getting sore. Still, he couldn't bring himself to stop, even for a minute.

The dog had no concept of time. The sky was beginning to lighten. He trotted up a long driveway. He kept to the grassy middle of the trail to give his paws a break from the hard ground. As he got closer to the building, he slowed his advance. He raised his nose. Sniffed to test the air.

He halted his advance. Sniffed again. And again. He had found the scent.

He lowered his nose and swept back and forth across the ground. His nose found something wet and sticky. He halted suddenly. Raised his head. Ran up the steps to the door. He paused long enough to sniff before jumping down. He circled the house.

Wagged his tail. Stopped.

This was the place. He was certain.

He barked. Quick-trotted to another side of the house. Barked again. Did the same until he covered all four sides with his bark.

A door slammed. Someone came out. It was a scent he didn't recognize. The human aimed a light around the yard.

Friday crouched to stay out of sight until the door slammed again. He circled the house to halt on each side in order to bark as loud as he could.

Satisfied, he retreated down the driveway to the street. He began to make his way back to the car and the grass and the building. He thought he recognized a distinctive whistling sound, but he was too far away to be sure. He quickened his pace anyway.

Once at the car, he got down on the grass on his stomach. He was exhausted. His feet were sore. He curled up and settled in and prepared to wait for his master to come for him.

SEVEN

Jim Nash gassed up the SUV.

Inside the stop'n'go, Luz scanned the warmers for road food. She returned with a couple of gas station burritos, as Jim called them, and some miscellaneous bagged treats. She had water, too.

"I don't know how you can eat that fake food, James. I would not be able to stomach it."

He grinned at Luz across the SUV. "Good American fast food, woman. What are you complaining about? Think of the time we're saving. It's either that, or a trip through a takeout lane with a lineup longer than the sidewalk."

She knew better than to argue with him. She once listened to Maddie tell tales of the man's fast-food preferences. Instead, she agreed. "Of course. You are right. Let us go." She got in and closed the door, eager to be back on the road.

"Are we ready? Before I forget, I put an MP5 beneath the spare tire in the back. I threw in two rails. You know. Just in case," he told her.

"That is good to know."

"To get to it fast you'll need to cut the cord securing the tire with a knife." He knew Luz carried one in each boot, and she was wearing her boots. He checked.

"You might as well climb into the back again. We have at least a couple of hours to go."

"I can drive if you want," Luz offered. "Perhaps you should sleep, too."

He didn't need to be asked twice. He climbed out and opened the door to the rear seat, where he stretched out. He was asleep almost before Luz pulled out of the massive truck stop.

Luz fiddled with the GPS and scrolled to their destination. Blue Springs. Of course, she never heard of it. She wondered how Jim settled on that place to try and meet up with missing Maddie.

Except, now the woman wasn't missing. Jim located her in a marina with some friends. Maddie went to try to find a missing girl that in the end turned out not to be missing.

Apparently, Maddie headed to the marina right away, before she knew the full story. That was all right with her. She, too, would have done the same for any of her friends.

Her friends. She didn't have many. James and Maddie. Emma. Nancy and Don Boyle and their daughter, Tricia. Not in any special order. She considered all of them to be good friends.

It wasn't long before the GPS showed the

turnoff coming up. She scrolled the screen, wanting to be certain of the name. Blue Springs. She called to James in the back.

"Santiago. We are here."

Alerted by Luz's voice, Jim looked out the window. The white FEMA trailers were long gone. From what he could tell in the dark, it looked as though the area was planted with grass.

"What street, James?" Luz asked.

The question brought him back from his reverie. "Turn left and follow it to a coffee shop on the right. It's probably closed now."

Jim's eyes went wide. "Park. Stop and park now."

Luz obeyed instantly. She went on full alert. She pulled her Model 71 and put in her lap as she slowed and steered the car to the side of the street. She doused the lights and turned off the ignition. "What is it? What do you see?"

"The headlights illuminated the yellow front of a car. Or at least the twin of Maddie's car. I think she's here. That's got to be her car."

Jim got out of the SUV. He put fingers to lips and a sharp, steady whistle pierced the night air. There was no answering bark. He crossed the street and bent to look inside. It was Maddie's car, all right. Where the hell was she? And where was Friday?

There was nothing they could do now. He got back into the SUV. "That's the car. We'll take turns every four hours. I'll go first. Friday doesn't appear to be here, either."

Luz powered the passenger seat-back and closed

her eyes. All the boring driving tired her. Knowing it was Maddie who was missing didn't help. She was emotionally exhausted, too.

"Wake me when it is my time."

EIGHT

The tow truck groaned to a halt beside the yellow car. Air brakes swooshed and locked. The driver got out. Walked around his truck. Tried a door on the car. It was locked. He walked back to his truck, repositioned it directly in front of the vehicle, and began lowering the deck.

The noise disturbed Friday. He snorted and stretched and jumped up behind the shrub. He poked his nose around it and saw a man at the car. He barked and ran full-tilt to the car. He placed himself between the man and his mistress's car. The man retreated to the truck and returned with a baseball bat.

Luz woke with a start. She exited the SUV and advanced toward the truck. She recognized a Mexican surname on the door. She addressed the man in Spanish. "You do not want to touch the dog, señor."

The man froze.

"If you hurt the dog, you will be in more trouble than you will know how to deal with. I will hunt down your family and kill them. I will burn your house down, and then I will hunt down your mother and father and kill them, too. You, I will leave alive to reap the consequences."

The man released the bat. It clunked to the ground. His voice wavered. "Sicario."

"Si. Ochoa. Pick up your bat and go away and you will be safe."

The man's teeth chattered. "You should move the car behind the coffee shop. There is space there."

"Gracias, señor. I will think about doing that."

Luz called to the dog. "Friday. Come. Jim is here."

Friday trotted beside Luz to the SUV. He looked up at her and snorted and woofed and licked at her fingers.

She bent to scratch an ear before banging on the SUV's window. "James. Friday is here," she announced.

He groaned and opened the door.

Friday made a half-hearted attempt to jump up, but he was too tired and sore.

Luz bent to help him, and he settled in beside Jim in the back seat.

"He needs food and water." She opened a bag of salty chips and poured a bottle of water into it. She lowered it to Friday. He licked and slopped and whined and drank his fill before returning his wet muzzle to Jim's lap.

"I think he is so tired for a reason, James. I think he has been out looking for Maddie. Do you think he could have found her?"

The dog whined and wagged his tail.

"Anything is possible, I guess. I want to be first in line to get into the coffee shop in a couple of hours, but first things first. I'd like to see if there's a waffle house around here somewhere. Friday needs to eat. And so do we."

"The tow truck driver suggested putting the car at the back of the coffee shop. Give me the keys."

Jim put in a call to Emma to ask about open restaurants in the area. She came back with one, complete with directions. When Luz returned from dropping off the car, the tired threesome headed off.

"When we're done eating, I'm going to take Friday back and put him on his long leash. Maybe he'll be able to sniff out Maddie."

Anxious Friday didn't want to wait. He worried in the back seat with his pacing and jumping up and whining in the confines of the back of the SUV.

"He knows something." He reached to pet the dog and scratch at an ear. "Friday. Food and water. Then Maddie."

The black dog barked, but his fussing didn't stop.

NINE

Maddie **was certain she** had heard a dog barking. It was too faint to know if it was Friday, but the sound, real or imagined, left her with some measure of hope.

She had little of that once she got a look around Billy-boy's basement in the light of dawn. It was a mess of clothes and bags and boxes and discarded shoes and tired household items. Billy-boy definitely needed a housekeeper.

Sunshine was beginning to filter through the barred windows. She could clearly see the staircase and climbed it one slow step at a time. She kept her ear cocked for sounds from beyond the door. There was nothing.

Unless it was soundproofed. She didn't think it was. There was no one upstairs.

She tried the door handle. It twisted, but she

couldn't shoulder the door open. She tried a couple of kicks, but she was forced to kick from two steps down. The kicks ended up fruitless. She lost her balance with the effort and almost tumbled down the steps.

Resigned, she returned to the basement. She slid boxes beneath windows to act as a step. The windows were all barred from the outside. Even if she broke the glass, she wouldn't have any progress. Then she remembered the barking dog.

She grabbed a handful of t-shirt and wrapped it around her fist. Thought better of it and found a discarded jean jacket. She made sure two metal buttons were on the outside and swung at the glass. It broke. She swung two more times to break all of it.

Satisfied, she moved to each of the windows and did the same. If there was a dog out there, and if it was her dog, she would know about it. She made sure to pick at as much glass as she could in case it was Friday. If he found her, he would be impatient to get to her. She didn't want him cutting his feet.

There wasn't anything else she could do but explore her surroundings. There were no chains. She opened a door and found a bathroom and used it. She caught herself before her head sank into her hands. She would be damned if she was going to feel sorry for herself until she got herself out of this dump.

And when she got out of the dump, she would have no need to feel sorry for anyone but Billy the hillbilly.

Damn him to hell.

She kicked herself for not at least sending off a text

to Jim to let him know where she was stopping. He would have insisted she keep right on going.

Come to think of it, that's what she should have done on her own. She cursed out loud at her stupidity. Not only had it put her in jeopardy, her dog was now in the same boat.

She roamed the basement in search of a container. If it was her dog. If it was Friday. Faithful Friday, who she left in the lurch on an empty sidewalk in Blue Springs. Without food or water.

TEN

Jim and Luz took up a four-top in the almost empty waffle house.

The server didn't bat an eye when she recognized the big black dog under the table. "Would your dog like some water?"

"He sure would. Is there any chance you have a large-size bowl? I'm going to be ordering food for him, too."

The woman with the name tag that said Jolene looked around the almost empty restaurant. "That should be all right. If we don't have a big bowl, would the biggest plate we have be okay?"

"Yes, thank you. That would be perfect."

"Is it all right if I pet your dog? He's gorgeous."

Jim bent to look down at the dog. "Did you hear that, Friday? Jolene thinks you're a handsome boy."

Friday's ears perked up. Jolene got down and

formed a fist with her hand. She held it in front of Friday.

He sniffed and snuffled. His tail flapped against the floor. Finally his pink tongue made contact, and she scratched an ear.

"You pass the test, Jolene. He likes you."

The server smiled, pleased as punch. She left her order book on the table and made for the sink to wash her hands.

"Did you see that, Luz? This is a good clean place."

Jim allowed Luz to order while he thought about what he might get for Friday.

"I'll have two over easy with wheat toast and jam. A separate triple order of nice crisp bacon in some tinfoil so we can take it away with us. Another separate order with two over hard, ham, and just a tiny wee bit of hash browns. Oh, and maybe four sausages, too, for more takeaway. We're watching his waistline."

Luz laughed.

The server expressed surprise and grinned. "Everyone's on a diet these days." She looked under the table. "I'll be back shortly, Friday."

Friday didn't look up. He was snoozing already.

Jjim said, "Look at him, Luz. He's exhausted. He needed help to get into the car."

Luz went behind the counter to refresh the water in the dog's bowl. Friday didn't bother with that, either. His breathing remained relaxed and even.

"How are we going to find Maddie, James? Your dog—"

"Friday was probably up all night. I don't think he was under a tree howling at the moon. I think he was out trying to track down his mistress. Look how exhausted he is."

Luz checked beneath the table and spotted Jim's sock feet. "He's laying on your feet."

Jim grinned across the table. "That's my boy. It's what he usually does with Maddie when he's feeling a little insecure. He'll be all right when the food comes. He'll be even better when we find her."

Jolene arrived with the plates. "I'll be right back with Friday's special. Say, we could make a menu item out of it, don't you think?" She returned and kneeled to place Friday's breakfast feast on the floor. The dog didn't move.

"He won't take it from you, Jolene," Jim said.

A look of disappointment appeared on Jolene's face.

"He's trained that way," Jim explained. "He doesn't take food from people he doesn't know. Well, okay, he takes it from little kids, but it's only when he gets permission. He likes to hear the little ones giggle when he nudges their hands and licks their little fingers."

The server guffawed. "I know some grown men just like that." Jolene placed Friday's tray on the table before leaving to go behind the counter. She bent and leaned over her elbows to watch the show. Jim cut everything up using a knife and fork. He sidelined two of the sausages for later.

Satisfied, Jim placed the dog's platter on the floor. Friday sighed and stretched and got up. He looked up at Jim, and across at the watching server.

"It's all for you, dog. You can thank that young lady after you finish it off."

Jolene watched in awe as the dog dug in. "I'm

thinking that is one spoiled dog."

Jim smiled. "Not really. We just tracked him down. He's been alone and up all night searching for his mistress. He's exhausted. He was without food and water the entire time. This is his treat before we go out and try to find her."

"Oh my goodness. Is there anything I can do?"

Luz brought out her phone and showed the woman a picture. "That's her? I know I haven't seen her in here. I work the entire shift every day. My husband owns the place and does the cooking."

A huge man walked up to stand beside Jolene. "Is that the special customer you were telling me about? He sure seems to like the grub. We should do an advert featuring him for sure."

Friday finished, burped, and moved to slurp from his water bowl.

"If you want to give him a little food, I saved a sausage for you, Jolene. You can give it to him in bits and then rub his chest. He'll remember you for the rest of his life. When he's finished, you can pat him."

Jim pushed his chair back and made sure Friday could see him handing over the sausage. "It's okay, Friday. Jolene is cool."

Friday gently and happily took the treats from Jolene's fingers, one by one.

"When you're done, could I trouble you for an envelope?" Jim asked.

While Jolene was away, Jim counted out ten hundred-dollar bills from the wad in his pocket. He caught Luz looking at him. "Do you think that's too much?"

"No, James. They probably know everyone in

town. They could be useful."

Unseen by Jolene, he tucked the cash into the envelope. He added one of his business cards.

"All right, dog, it's time to go to work."

He slid the chair back and stood up. He grabbed one of the diner's cards from near the register and walked outside. Jolene followed them.

"Could we get a picture with Friday?" she asked. She held up a camera.

Jim called to the dog. "Picture time, Friday. Go sit with Jolene and be a good boy."

Friday scampered up the steps. He nuzzled Jolene's neck with a cold nose. She laughed and put her arm around him. Jim snapped the picture and handed the camera back.

"Can I take one with you and your friend?" Jolene asked.

Luz cleared her throat and took the opportunity to head for the SUV. Jim called to the dog. "Time to go. Say goodbye, Friday."

Friday woofed and scampered after Luz. Jim made a diplomatic exit and followed the pair. The last thing he saw was Jolene on the steps of the diner. The envelope was in her hands. She waved it while calling her goodbyes to Friday.

"I got some cooking oil for Friday's feet, James. I think he needs it," Luz said.

Jim held open the back door to let Friday jump up. The dog was obviously feeling much better.

"You better not let M-a-d-d-i-e find out. She'll think you want to steal her dog. Hand it over." He grinned at Luz. "Thanks for thinking of that. I never would have."

ELEVEN

Jim looked across the SUV at Luz. "We can use those two if we need them." He meant Jolene and her husband. Luz didn't appear appeased, but she nodded.

"We are here for one thing, James. It is to find Maddie. When we do, I am going to talk to her about the proper way to do these things."

Already Jim could hear a lecture coming, and from Luz, no less. She wasn't a happy camper. He wondered if he should mention her recent foray into Mexico to remind her that none of them was perfect.

Luz went on. "I know I am not the best, either. I went to Mexico on my own to complete a task. Perhaps I should have told you about it. Perhaps not. But still, concerning Maddie, she should have told you. She is your partner."

Well, there went his mention of Mexico out the

window. Speaking of which, he cracked the back window for Friday. "I know. I'm pretty sure no one is going to be more embarrassed by all of this more than Maddie. Maybe we can just forget about it for now and concentrate on our task."

He parked across the street from the coffee shop where they had discovered Maddie's car. "Will you please call Emma and give her an update? I'm sure she's worrying about all of us by now."

Luz grinned. "I did that while you were sleeping last night, James. I will call her again now that we have Friday and some hope for finding Maddie."

"Thank you. Now here's the thing. I'm pretty sure that d-o-g is going to jump past me and start heading down the road before I can get a handle and a leash on him. I do not want that to happen. If it does, we'll be chasing after him the entire time."

Jim leaned over the back seat and reached for his bag on the floor. "I don't want Friday to cost us our element of surprise." He pulled out the long leash. "Friday. Come."

While he waited for the dog to worm his way from the back of the SUV to the rear seat, he explained how he wanted to use him. "I think he found something last night. I want to get him outside. He's going to want to run as fast as he can. I can keep up for a while, but there won't be any corralling him by a long shot. You're going to have to take over for me before I lose both my lungs."

Jim handed over the tinfoil containing the bacon. "He likes this stuff. We can use it to treat him for being a good boy when he slows down. I hope we have enough of it."

Luz grinned. "You mean you hope he slows down some of the time."

Friday jumped to the ground. His ears faced forward and his tail stretched straight back. He was in full tracking mode.

Luz waited for the pair to get ahead of her.

Friday strained at the leash dragging Jim behind him.

Jim allowed the long leash to play out as slowly as he could. He had difficulty holding the dog back as he continued to bound forward.

He called to Friday often. The dog ignored him for the most part. Exasperated, Jim called and whistled. Friday slowed and waited for the man to catch up. "Good boy, Friday." He handed off a taste of bacon and bent to pat the dog.

"That was almost like being at home with Emma, wasn't it? Now slow down. I'm a tired man."

Friday barked. Jim knew there was no way he would be able to slow the dog. He called to Luz. "Your turn. I need a break."

He handed off the leash and took his turn behind the wheel. Friday dashed off. He came to the end of the leash and looked back. He recognized Luz and slowed.

"Well I'll be damned. That darned dog slows for women."

Jim wasn't fooled for long. Friday's nose tested Luz's hand. He snorted and took off, albeit at a much slower pace.

"I saw that!"

Luz laughed. "Well, you did tell me the bacon was a treat. I decided to treat him if he slowed down."

TWELVE

Hinges creaked. **Maddie looked** up the stairs to see Billy in the open door, highlighted by the kitchen light. His long shadow spilled down the stairs, halting short of the bottom step. He reached to turn on the basement lights. They illuminated the work she did to rearrange the mess left behind by his previous prisoner.

If there was one. It might only be her imagination.

"I see you've been busy. Get down on your knees and put your hands behind your head."

Maddie didn't see any way out. She did as she was told. The handcuffs Billy waved rattled. Broken glass crunched underfoot. Her work on the windows didn't go unnoticed.

"You wasted your time. We're too far out in the country for anyone to hear you."

That was probably true. If the dog came back, she would be able to find out if it was Friday. There was that chance, at least. Friday would listen to her. He would do what she told him to do. Maybe, just maybe, she could get the dog to attack her kidnapper if he stepped outside.

But then what? She would still be stuck in the basement. She would starve without help. Unfortunately, as faithful a dog as he was, Friday was incapable of getting past a door.

"Where are we going? I'm hungry. Can I have something to eat? Could you pick up some food? Maybe a couple of plain hamburgers with bacon? I'd like some water, too, please." It was worth a try.

"You'll see when we get there. Now shut up." Billy cuffed her to his wrist and pulled her after him up the stairs and outside to the truck. He opened the driver's door and slid past to let her get behind the wheel. He handed over the keys. "I'll tell you where to go."

He directed her to a restaurant parking lot. It was west of downtown. He took the keys, unfastened his cuff, and attached it to the steering wheel. "Don't go away." He laughed and got out.

"Are you going to get something to eat?"

Her tormentor walked off without a word.

Maddie sat back in the seat. Her mind raced. She looked around. There were no other cars in the lot. Billy parked far enough away that any sound she made would go unnoticed. The windows were up anyway. She twisted in the seat and rearranged herself in a window facing the diner. If anyone bothered to look, they might see her.

Her thoughts raced back to the basement and the crowbar. She found it beneath a pile of discarded clothes. It was sturdy and strong. Not too long. Just maybe she could use it on the window bars. She didn't know if they were fastened on the outside of the house. Maybe they were mounted in cement. If that was the case—

The truck door opened. She gasped, startled. She had been so engrossed in thinking about her escape, she didn't notice Billy's return from the diner.

He climbed in. She caught a glance of a woman inside the diner, looking out at them. The door closed. Billy unlocked the handcuff, and she was once again attached to him. What was the phrase? Attached at the waist? That didn't apply in this case. That was more voluntary, between friends. Billy was no friend.

"We're going home."

The overpowering smell of the hamburgers gave her hope. "Did you get something to drink? I like root beer."

Her hopes were dashed when he refused her request. She was hoping he'd mention water.

"Shut up and drive, woman."

On purpose, she made a wrong turn and pointed the truck toward the downtown. Billy cursed and grabbed the wheel. The handcuff got in the way and the truck steered toward the curb. It bounced over it before he could correct and then bounced back.

"Dammit. Do what I tell you."

Her attempt got them off course. For an instant, she thought she saw a big black dog being walked by a woman. They were too far away to be sure. Still, it could have been Friday. By the time she got the truck back to Billy's, she convinced herself it was Friday. But who was the woman?

Of course. Emma. It had to be Emma. But where was Jim? She cursed out loud for not sending him a text, at least. She cursed out loud a second time for allowing herself to get trapped like this. Apparently, situational awareness wasn't one of her strong points.

"Are you going to let me eat when we get inside? I'm starving."

The hamburger smell overwhelmed her. It took her mind off of her circumstances, at least. She would have plenty of time to feel sorry for herself once the food was gone. "Will we be eating upstairs or down?"

It was a feeble attempt to make him feel like he would be including her. It didn't work. He shoved her toward the basement door. She bounced off of it into the wall. He handed her one of the bags and undid the handcuff. "Get down there. And don't make noise or else."

Maddie didn't ask, Or else what? She figured she already knew.

THIRTEEN

Jim looked at the number on his ringing phone and didn't recognize it. He answered anyway. Jolene didn't give him an opportunity to talk.

"The woman in the picture is in our parking lot in a half-ton. The man who owns the truck is sitting in the restaurant right now. His name is Billy Denver. He'll probably be another ten minutes."

"Can you get out to the truck?"

"No. He'll see me. Do you want me to call the police?" Jolene asked.

"No. No police. We'll handle this our way."

"I understand. Hurry. I can't keep him here much longer."

"Don't make him suspicious, Jolene. Let him leave if he wants to go."

Jim honked the horn and drove up to Luz. "Jolene called." He looked at the dog and bit his tongue. You-know-who is in a truck in the restaurant parking lot. She says she knows who has her."

"Do you want us to come with you?"

"No. Keep going with Friday. She wanted to call the police. I let her know we would handle it our way."

Jim turned the car around and made for the restaurant. By the time he arrived, the truck and Maddie were gone. He rushed to confront Jolene and her husband.

"Billy Denver. That's his name. He's a local crazy. Always a trouble-maker. He's got some girlfriend that's an inmate. She's in a wheelchair. In for life, apparently, too. He seems convinced she's going to get out on an early parole. At least that's what he said just now."

Fiona Lubinski. Dammit to hell. Her again. He didn't say a word to Jolene about recognizing the woman. "Thanks for calling me. Where does Billy live? Do you know if he has any guns?"

Damn. He didn't know if Luz was armed. He pulled out his phone. He didn't have Luz's burn phone in it. He cursed his stupidity and put in a call to Emma to tell her to warn Luz.

"Where does this guy live? He's a local, I take it."

Jolene spread a napkin on the counter and drew a rough map. She X'd the spot and wrote the street name. "That's roughly where he lives. The house is back from the road. I don't know if it will be in your GPS. It's out in the country by just a bit."

"Thanks, you two. We appreciate it." The envelope with the thousand in it wouldn't be enough if he found Maddie thanks to them.

Jim rushed back to the SUV and tore out of the parking lot. He slowed only enough to dictate the address to the car's nav system. It accepted it and pinged and a red circle surrounded the location. "What do you know? I'm thinking Luz might just about be there already."

He wasn't certain. They covered a lot of ground, thanks to Friday's relentless pace. Still, the dog had to be slowing down. And Luz was probably close to exhaustion, too. Consequently, his foot didn't waste time on the empty space beneath the gas pedal. He filled it on every straight stretch he found.

He caught up to the exhausted pair on a side road in the general vicinity of Billy Denver's place. He figured they were a mile north.

"I'm going to call Emma again. We need to get her to give us a satellite view of the place. And I'm damned if I'm ever going to buy a cheap phone again. I never realized how much we need them now that we need them."

Friday got a drink for his efforts. Luz snacked on salted beef. Jim brought out restaurant hamburgers for the lot of them.

Luz took great pleasure in feeding Friday his burger.

"How much bacon do you have left?"

"I have been stingy with it. He seems happy so far."

Friday nuzzled Luz's fingers, searching for more. She shook her head and told him No more. "I think he likes me now."

Jim grinned, knowing that Friday liked anyone he

could beg, borrow, or steal food from. He didn't let on to Luz.

Emma's voice came back over the speaker. "When you come to the driveway, it's looks to be half a mile or so to a house. Gravel with a grass patch in the center. It's all open ground, except for a patch of bush blocking the view to the front of the house."

Jim looked at Luz and nodded. "That's good information, Emma. We can make use of it."

She went on. "There appears to be a similar patch at the back. A couple of small outbuildings, probably storage. No garage. There looks to be plenty of junkers in the yard. And junk, too."

Luz was looking more hopeful after hearing about the cover.

"You've made our day, Emma," Jim told her. "Did I mention we moved the car off the street and parked it behind the coffee shop?"

"The one where I used to work? I loved that place. The people were so friendly. All it takes is one rotten apple, and we seem to have found more than that. I can't believe we're still dealing with Fiona. Damn that woman."

"That's the place. Friday has done a bang-up job of scouting. He's tuckered both Luz and I out with his enthusiasm. Get back to us if you think of anything else. And thanks for your help."

FOURTEEN

Jim and Luz knew where they were going. They knew how they'd get there. They had the expertise. They had the equipment. They didn't know what would be waiting.

Would Billy Denver be on alert? Would he be thinking there was someone coming for him? Did he know the dog was with Maddie when he took her? Was he alone in this, or did he have help?

"I still can't believe that dog tracked down his mistress. I have to admit, I'm overwhelmed. Friday, you are a very good boy. Your mistress will be so proud of you."

Jim unrolled a piece of sausage and held it out.

Friday bit it a couple of times and it disappeared. His tail wagged for more.

"That's all. Good boy."

His attention went to Luz. "How do you think

we should attack our problem? Is she even there? Is Denver back from the restaurant with his trophy yet? And what the hell was he doing parading her around the restaurant and bragging about her?"

"We only know what we know, James. The man has Maddie."

Hearing the name, Friday barked.

"Sorry, Friday. Jolene helped us confirm he has her, thanks to the sighting in the parking lot. We know where he lives, again thanks to Jolene. We think Friday followed the scent, or whatever he did, to the kidnapper's place. So he knows where she is. What more do we need?"

Jim knew Luz wanted to charge in and kick ass. If that happened, there wouldn't be any taking names. Billy wouldn't get out alive. Nor would anyone else she discovered in the building if they were a party to Maddie's abduction.

"Luz?"

She looked at him.

"We can't kill him. Or them, if there's more than one. This isn't Mexico. We'll go to prison. Jolene and her husband know we're looking for Billy. I left my card, remember? The police would find out who we were instantly."

He wasn't sure if it was a look of disappointment or relief that crossed Luz's face.

"We'll walk up to the house. The information Emma passed along regarding the bushes should be good. Now here's the thing. If I leave Friday in the car, he'll tear it apart. Piece by piece. I can't have that. He could hurt himself. Maddie would never forgive me. I know you think it's silly, but that's the way it is."

"I understand. Let us go find Friday's señora."

That was one word the dog didn't know. At least he wasn't charging forward more than usual.

He drove up and down the main road, hoping to find a place they could leave the car and remain out of sight. He thought better of it when he realized Billy wouldn't know it from a bus.

Maddie would, though, and if Billy got ahead of them, she would see it. It would leave her with some hope.

"What do you think?"

Luz said, "That is good. We still have to get to the house. Will you be able to keep Friday quiet? Is that possible, given that it is his señora in the house?"

Luz sounded happy so far.

"I'm hoping the surrounding bushes will provide cover. I think you should take the back side. That will set you on your own course. Friday should be a lot more calm with me. Easier to control, too." I hoped. I didn't say it.

There was one more thing. "We can't kill him," I reminded Luz. "We need to keep him alive. Is that clear?"

Luz's response was terse. "Si. Entiendo. You already told me."

FIFTEEN

Maddie's kidnapper had **over**-tightened the handcuffs. It cut off her circulation. She rubbed at her wrist. Feeling slowly returned. Her hands shook as she opened the bag and looked in. Just what she needed. Two burgers and fries. And bacon! Friday would be so happy. If it was Friday.

She looked around the basement for a box. She dragged it into position for a table and settled in for lunch. Random thoughts intruded on her meal. She felt she was making some progress with Billy. Didn't think he was going to kill her. At least, not right away. She took little comfort from that.

What was he doing with her? Was she a prize he could tell Fiona about the next time he visited the woman? What was he going to do with her once that was accomplished? She was pretty sure where Fiona stood once she learned Billy had a prisoner, and that prisoner was her. She wouldn't be long for this world if Billy bowed to the woman's twisted wishes.

She didn't eat the last burger. She kept some of the fries, too. If the dog came back, she'd have something to pass through the bars.

She remembered the crowbar. Retrieved it from beneath the pile of clothes. Tested the weight. Could she keep it hidden close enough that she could haul it out and use it to thump Billy?

If she tried to pry the bars, it would surely make too much noise. He would come investigating. And that thought led her back to batting him on the head. She would take great pleasure in doing that.

Refreshed by the food, she began to feel a bit like a daredevil. She climbed up on a cardboard box full of clothes. Unsteady on her feet, she reached through the bars and felt with her fingers for whatever was securing it to the house. She recognized some were screws. Most were nails.

At first, she pried gently. Wanted to get the crowbar in place for maximum force. Got annoyed when it wasn't as easy as she thought it would be. Almost gave up. Persevered until she had the first nail out.

She tried one of the screws next and immediately discovered they would not be so easy. The screw screeched in the wood. She held her breath. Listened. No movement upstairs. She repeated the motion. More screeching as it pulled at the wood. It popped all of a sudden, and the bar clattered out of her grip.

Right away she knew she should have pulled a long sock over the pry bar. She got down from the box and went hunting. It took her five minutes in the mess of clothes, but she found one. She almost jumped for joy before pulling the woolen sock over the crowbar. It would be silent but for the screws and nails she forced out of the wood.

Her thoughts returned to the woman walking the dog. It had to be a stranger. But that wasn't possible. Friday wouldn't go with a stranger. If it was Friday. She went back to thinking it was Emma. It had to be.

That, or her mind was playing tricks. Frustrated, she sighed.

Where was Jim?

SIXTEEN

Billy Denver checked the basement door. He grabbed the knob and twisted, hard, testing. Pulled at the padlock and hasp. Nothing gave way. Satisfied, he made for his truck. He was already late for his promised visit with Fiona. He didn't want to disappoint the woman by missing even once.

The black SUV on the side of the main road didn't concern him. He ignored it and sped past. He almost missed the turn into the prison parking lot. He braked hard and straightened and finally came to a stop. He ran to the gate, got admitted, and passed through the metal detector. He held out his arms, and the guard scanned him with the wand.

"You almost didn't make it this time. She's probably wondering why you stood her up.

Fiona Lubinski looked up to check the clock in the visitor area. She was rolling her chair to the exit when she saw Billy reflected in the window. The fool was huffing and puffing. He had a huge grin pasted on his face. The grin didn't improve his looks.

"What's the big deal? I waited for you, and you're late."

He almost screamed across the table at her. "I got her. I got her."

He looked around. None of the guards appeared to hear or notice his glee.

Fiona narrowed her eyes and looked across the table. The fool looked like he was having a fit. Perhaps he was the one that should be on the inside.

"What are you talking about, Billy?"

He would flop on the floor like a fish if he kept that up. His wide eyes and nodding head betrayed him.

"What news have you brought?"

"I got her."

There it was again. "Spill your guts, man. I'm not a fortune teller." How the hell was she supposed to know what was going on? She hadn't seen him since last month.

"That woman. You know. That woman. That woman." He could barely speak. "Maddie. Maddie. You know the one. I got her. I got Maddie. She's in my basement."

Fiona's gaze fixed on him. Her jaw went slack. She didn't believe him. Her eyes narrowed. She glanced toward the guards. Her mouth twisted.

Should she believe him?

"How did it happen?"

Billy's eyes bored into hers. He bounced on the chair. "I spotted her in the coffee shop a couple of days ago. I remembered who she was. I forced her out the back door. She's in the basement. She's in my basement."

"How do you know it's her? It's been a while."

Billy's head tilted back. "It's her. I checked. I know it's her." His fist pumped the air.

"Calm down, Billy. The guards will get suspicious," she warned him.

Fiona's brow creased. She still didn't believe him. He should have brought a picture. She motioned for him to come closer. "I'll try to get a call out later. I might be able to bribe someone. You can let me talk to her. That should prove one way or the other whether it's Maddie. What's she doing out here all alone? Did you ask?

Of course he didn't ask. He was too busy gloating, but he wouldn't admit that.

"I haven't had time. I've been too busy."

Billy could tell her smile was fake, but he didn't care any more. He would show her as soon as she called.

The bell went off, announcing the end of visiting hours.

Billie pushed Fiona to her exit door and walked off to his own. He was still pumped. If Fiona didn't get it, it wasn't his problem.

Billy drove home thinking about what he would do to Maddie once he proved to Fiona he had her. It was all her fault Fiona was in a wheel chair in the first place. Her and that damned dog. If the dog hadn't lunged at Fiona, driving her back against the trailer, Fiona might still be walking.

He steered the truck into his driveway on a high.

SEVENTEEN

Jim **waited until Billy's** truck was out of sight before he and Luz got out of the SUV to check their gear. Each went through their separate routines until it was time to check the other's equipment.

"I'm going to hightail it all the way to the end of the driveway. If Maddie is there, we'll get her."

He didn't consider for a second that she wasn't.

He slapped Luz's backpack. She was good.

"I'm glad you're here, Luz. I know I can depend on you at times like these."

"Gracias, Santiago. I have the same for you. Let us go."

Jim raced the car down the long gravel driveway. He locked the brakes and skidded to a halt feet from the steps to Billy's ramshackle house.

"Emma was right. The place is a junk pile. Friday. Out." He opened the door.

Friday was only too eager to get his freedom. He scrambled out and ran around the house, barking.

Maddie heard the commotion. Heard the tires skidding in the driveway. Was he back already? It was the barking. The dog was back.

"Friday? Is that you?"

The dog halted at a window. A part of the heavy mesh screen was pried off. The space was big enough that he could stick his head in. He whined.

Maddie's hand reached to comfort him. "It's okay, Friday. It's okay. I'm okay, too. I'm okay."

She passed a bit of the hamburger she had saved through the opening. The dog ignored her and withdrew.

"Don't go. Don't go, Friday. Come back." Panicky, she recognized a man's voice.

"We don't want to be seen to turn down food, woman, but we've eaten already, thank you very much."

Jim's head replaced Friday's. "Have you finished looking at that report yet, dear?"

Maddie screamed. "Cripes. I thought for a second you were Billy."

"Never mind that. How did you get the bars loose?"

She disappeared to get the crowbar. "With this."

She passed it out the window and Jim used it to pry the remaining screen off the window. It slipped to the grass and landed with a thud.

"Come on, woman. Your chariot awaits." He heaved and pulled and Maddie came out of the window and landed on top him.

Friday jumped on the pair and licked and snuffled and woofed and barked.

"All right. The play date is over. Luz is going to replace you. I tried to talk her out of it, but once she gets something in her head—"

Maddie interrupted. "I think I'd like to join her."

"Bad idea. Now let's get going. You have a report to finish."

Luz approached the pair from behind. "Apparently, you do. Jim has been harping on it the entire time you have been missing. Even Friday has commented on it. She reached to slap the dog's side for emphasis, grinning the whole time."

Jim laughed nervously. If Maddie only knew. "We had a meeting where we decided you need a break, Maddie. Now give Luz your clothes."

"What? Why?"

"Because I am going to be you," Luz said. "Your shirt and hoodie should be enough. Hurry, please."

The women traded tops. Luz dropped her backpack through the basement window. It clunked onto the floor. Luz followed.

Jim lined up the bars and replaced some nails to make it look as though it was still in place.

"Don't forget to give her the crowbar." Maddie held it out for Jim to pass through the basement window."

"She's not going to kill him, is she?" Maddie asked. She was more than familiar with Luz's cold-blooded nature.

"I asked her as nicely as I could not to do that, but she didn't promise," Jim said.

Maddie sighed. "I can never tell when you're kidding about that woman."

The sound of glass breaking filtered past the open window. "What's she doing?"

"She works best in the dark."

Luz called out. "I left him with one light to do his job. I will see you back at the restaurant. Or I will call when Billy Denver is done and you can come and get me."

Billy Denver's truck and the SUV met and passed on the county road. There was no sign of recognition.

EIGHTEEN

Billy Denver's truck fishtailed as he left the county road and turned onto the gravel driveway. He counter-steered and the truck straightened. Tires kicked up the gravel until he was forced to brake and skid to a halt on the grass in front of his house.

"I've got her. I've got her," he called out.

He was almost singing Maddie's name as he jumped out of the truck and ran for the locked front door. At the top of the steps, he turned for a quick look down the driveway to make sure no one followed him. Satisfied, he turned the key, entered, and closed and locked the door behind him.

He poured two cups of coffee, added cream and sugar, and got out his key for the padlock on the basement door. He unlocked it, flipped on the basement lights, and returned to the kitchen counter, where he picked up the coffee cups before making his way downstairs.

His phone rang, interrupting his journey. Distracted, he set the coffee cups down at the top of the stairs and answered it.

It was Fiona, and she was hopping mad.

A barrage of questions greeted him, none of which he had any answers for. He sputtered into his phone in a feeble attempt to get the woman to understand what he was doing. She wouldn't listen.

"You'll see, Fiona. You'll see. Do you want to talk to her?"

That shut her up. She was obviously considering his offer. He held his breath in anticipation.

"Yeah. Let me talk to that witch."

"You won't be disappointed, I promise." Billy was so consumed with pleasing Fiona he didn't notice some of the lights were out in the basement.

He stepped down. A foot caught in a pile of clothes and he tumbled into the woman's arms.

"Thanks for catching me. Someone wants to talk to you." He found his balance and held out the phone.

That was his first mistake.

It was also Billy's last.

NINETEEN

Luz sat up. Listened. Recognized the sound of gravel crunching beneath tires. The man was here.

She stood up and stretched to get blood to return to muscles cramped from sitting. The job had become a matter of waiting him out. She was good at that. She had plenty of practice at her former occupation in Mexico.

She allowed her mind to wander for only a second. Caught herself. Realized she was getting too soft in her new country with her new friends.

Luz reached for her backpack. Made sure it was at the foot of the stairs, behind the first step.

She checked her belt for the holstered Model 71. Even after all these years, she confirmed it would be an easy reach with her left hand. Repeated the motion again.

The door at the top of the stairs opened, throwing a beam of light all the way to the bottom. The light formed a shadow.

A phone rang, and the shadow disappeared.

The man returned and began walking down the steps. Still talking. Not paying attention. At the bottom, he stumbled. \

Luz reached to steady him and then withdrew.

He continued talking into the phone.

Luz was starting to wonder what was going on. Why was Billy so confident there was nothing awaiting him? He had kidnapped a woman. A woman who, apparently, had been the cause of the demise of his girlfriend.

Why hadn't Maddie done anything?

She remembered the crowbar the woman used to partially loosen the window bars. She could have used that on Billy.

Billy squinted into the darkened basement. "Hang on, Fiona."

Absorbed as he was in his phone conversation, he forgot the woman was beside him. "Where did you get to?" he asked.

They were the last words out of his mouth.

Luz shifted to Billy's left.

Her right arm pulled back across her chest.

She struck up and out.

Billy recognized something was wrong. It was already too late. The edge of the hand struck his throat head-on. Billy's last-second attempt to duck out of the way failed.

The phone dropped to the floor. He clutched at his throat with both hands. Wheezed and tried to inhale past his windpipe. He fell to his knees.

Luz reached for a shoulder to steady him. "Give me the phone."

Billy didn't recognize the voice. His wild eyes looked at Luz. He had no idea who she was. He gestured to the floor.

Luz picked up the phone.

"Listen to me, Fiona. Your boyfriend is in dire need of an ambulance. I have been told you are in a wheelchair thanks to Maddie and her dog."

She drew the pistol from its holster. Pulled back the action. "He will live or die depending on your answer."

Luz remembered she wasn't supposed to kill Billy. "If you ever bother anyone related to Maddie and Jim and even their dog Friday, Lobo will come for you. Entiendes? Do you understand?"

She handed the phone to Billy. "I suggest you call for help now."

Two shots rang out.

Billy screamed.

With no sense of what was happening, Fiona screamed. No one heard her.

Billy dropped to the floor. He cradled his knees with both hands and pulled them to his chest.

Luz took the phone and made her way upstairs. She used it one last time to call 911. She left a terse message with the operator before she hung up.

She wiped the phone, tossed it down the steps and began jogging across the open field toward the restaurant.

TWENTY

Maddie checked the clock over the restaurant's pass-through for the hundredth time. She could only tell Jim about how Billy Denver had trapped her so many times before enough was enough. Besides, she thought the story through while she was sitting in Denver's basement. She wasn't happy she had allowed herself to be caught like a fish in a tank.

"Shouldn't Luz be here by now?"

She was concerned about her. She pushed her chair back from the restaurant's four-top and got up.

Friday got up with her. He hadn't left her side since she crawled out of the basement where he found her.

"Go ahead and look. I'll wait here in case she shows up. Don't forget to take a phone this time," Jim said.

Maddie gave him a dirty look.

"And turn it on, please?"

Exasperated, Maddie turned to him. "Yes master. Your wish is my command."

Even so, she knew he was right.

Maddie held the door for Friday. He waited at the top of the diner's steps for her, and then walked beside her all the way to the car. The dog jumped in and made his way to the passenger seat.

"All right, good boy Friday. Just where did that woman of ours get to?"

An ambulance sped by with siren and flashing lights activated. "Oh-oh. I think I know where he's headed. Let's follow and see what comes our way."

In ten minutes, the pair had Luz in the back seat.

Friday jumped into the back to greet her with a wet nose and a lick.

"How did it go?" Maddie wanted to ask Luz if she killed Billy. She knew better. She went for the indirect approach instead.

"Billy has been taken care of. He won't bother you again. Neither will Fiona, his former friend."

Luz sensed what Maddie wanted to know. "He is alive, or the ambulance wouldn't be on the way."

So she heard the siren, too. Good to know. "I believe you," Maddie said.

She did, too.

TWENTY-ONE

The trio thanked Jolene for her help and said their goodbyes.

Even Friday got in a secret finger lick when Jolene surreptitiously offered him a bit of bacon.

Maddie heard the smacking lips and witnessed the wagging tail. She admonished the dog with a grin on her face.

"Friday. I saw that. Do you have a new bestie?"

He woofed, but refused to admit anything.

Jim said, "Would you like Luz to drive your car back? You and your favorite dog can stretch out in the back seat and get some rest."

She considered on the walk to the car. "I think Friday and I would like to go back in my car. It will be our penance for not paying attention and being unaware of our surroundings."

Maddie was embarrassed to admit it. She knew

Luz would never make that mistake.

Before she could go on, Luz interrupted. "I think I should drive your car home, Maddie. There are some things I still need to do."

"Are you sure, Luz?"

"Yes. I am sure. I have to have to make a stop at the towing company. There is something I need to check on."

Maddie didn't ask more questions.

She led Friday off to do his business before she let him jump in ahead of her. She stretched out on the leather seat.

Friday sat on the floor beside her.

"I'm exhausted. Don't bug us until we're home. One more thing. Your report is on our kitchen table. I have more notes to make. If you have complaints, take them to HR.

As though to back her up, Friday woofed."

"Well. I guess I've been told," Jim said.

Hours passed before Jim became concerned for Luz. She still wasn't back. He heard steps coming up the stairs and looked out his office window. Maddie's yellow car wasn't in its usual spot.

"What happened? You said you were going to visit the towing company."

"I did. I decided the car needed to be destroyed. I set fire to it. It is all good now," Luz said. She set the VIN plate on the desk.

"Maddie loved that little car."

Luz didn't look upset. "I will tell her when she gets up. She can buy another one."

"Speaking of telling, is there any chance you've made a decision on moving into Anya's former apartment?" Jim asked.

Luz stretched out on the office sofa. Jim opened the closet and handed her a pillow and blanket. "I have not made a decision yet. There are some things I need to discuss with Nancy first. You will understand."

"That's fine. Take as long as you need. If I can help, all you have to do is let me know, all right?"

Steps crashed down the stairs from the third floor. Emma stuck her head past the door. She waved her cell phone. "What the hell? Can't you guys pick up a phone and let a woman know everyone is safe? Where's Maddie? Where's Friday?"

"Don't panic. She's out walking her favorite dog before they both collapse into bed. Do you recall how I always talk about how she won't allow Friday into bed? Well, I'm thinking Friday will be there by the time I climb in. If I'm lucky, there'll be room for me with that pudgy, lazy, no-good dog of hers taking up all the room."

Maddie and Friday stuck their heads into the office. "Or for crying out loud, Nash. Are you looking for sympathy or what? Get your rear end upstairs and into bed with both of us."

Jim, hardly a man to say no to his woman and her dog, obeyed instantly. He trotted up the stairs ahead of both. He called down to Emma and Luz.

"I'll see you both tomorrow."

Luz got up and reached for the coffee pot on top of the cabinet.

"That's stale. I made it hours ago," Emma told

her.

"It will be fine, I am sure. There is something I want to talk about."

Luz hesitated. Emma didn't say anything. "I have been asked if I would like to live here. Is it a good place? What is it like with Jim and Maddie and her dog?"

Emma took a moment to breathe before she replied. "Well. I'm happy here. I consider Jim and Maddie to be family. Like all families, it can sometimes be a bit much. But then, that's what the door is for. I close it and lock it and off I go to work."

"What about Friday? Is he a good dog?"

"Friday? I think he's wonderful. I can't get enough of him. If I could, I'd run away with him and feed him all the bacon and toast and jam he could eat. Except—" Emma hesitated.

"Except what?" Luz asked.

"Except what? Maddie would be forced to hunt me down."

The women broke into laughter.

"Jim wouldn't be far behind. Tricia would be wanting him to bring her along on the hunt, even though she has Lola. Nancy would track us all down. And Don would have a BOLO out on all of us in record time."

More laughter echoed through the building. "Especially when Boyle found out it was me." Emma couldn't hold back the grin.

Luz raised an eyebrow. "I think there is a story there."

"Yes, there is. And I don't have time to tell it tonight. I have to work an early shift tomorrow."

About the author

Peter Duke is a Canadian author. He resides and writes in a small college town in the Province of Ontario, Canada.

Aviator. Fire pilot. Motorcycle rider. Vagabond. Drifter. Trouble-maker. Jack of all trades and master of none. Peter has been riding and writing about the places he's been and the people he's seen for more than a few years. Some of his writing is factual; some of it isn't. Peter likes to leave it up to the reader to determine the lies that might be the truth.

pxduke.com

peterxduke@gmail.com

Police Detective Jim Nash has a flawless career in a northern big-city police department until all of a sudden, he doesn't. He proves them all wrong, is re-instated, and stays in only long enough to collect his pension.

Print books

Jim Nash
Jim Nash The Beginning
Gun Crazy
Gun Crazy 2
Gun Crazy 3
Fallen Angels
Last Stop to Nowhere
Revenge is Justice
Escape / Forget Me Not
Wedding Bell Blues / Breakdown
Mexico Time
No Free Ride / Gone
LOBO
Stealing America
Blame It on Djibouti
No Escape
Trouble in Paradise
Nash & Delaney Collide

Harry Delaney Adventures
Dead Reckoning
Lie Cheat Steal
Uncharted
Go-Around
Sand Storm
Harry Delaney Collection

Frank Ross Biker Tales
No Way Out
Bad Girls
Bank Robber Dames

Other
The Last President

Check out all six books of the Harry Delaney Adventure series. Find out why Harry makes his way from the North African desert to the Mexican Baja. Discover how he ends up having a triumphal return to the deserts of North Africa.

Jim Nash Read Order

JIM NASH

Jim Nash The Beginning
Pirate Cay
Thrill Kill Jill
Greetings From Key West
Lost Paradise
No Angels
Mexico Gamble
No Picnic
Fallen Angels
Vendetta
A Girl's Best Friend
Dead End
No Harbor
Dog Days
Startup Blues
Last Stop To Nowhere / The Last
Goodbye
Revenge Is Justice
Escape
Wedding Bell Blues
Snap Brim Fedora Caper
Breakdown
Little Girl Lost
Forget Me Not
All The Glitter
Mexico Time
Partners In Crime
Shop Till You Drop
Lobo
No Free Ride
Gone
Stealing America
Blame It on Djibouti
No Escape
Trouble in Paradise
Nash & Delaney Collide

SEASONAL

Trick or Treat
Helping Santa

JIM NASH INVESTIGATES

The Snap Brim Fedora Caper
The Lady in White
The Lady in Yellow

www.ingramcontent.com/pod-product-compliance
Lightning Source LLC
Chambersburg PA
CBHW010552170726
48285CB00011B/2876